THE USBORNE BOOK OF
SUPERPUZZLES

MAP & MAZE PUZZLES

CODES & CIPHERS

LOGIC PUZZLES

Series Editor: Gaby Waters
Assistant Editor: Michelle Bates

Puzzle checkers: Harriet Castor, Christina Hopkinson,
Rachel Bladon, Richard Dungworth and Rachael Robinson

MAP & MAZE PUZZLES

Sarah Dixon

Illustrated by Radhi Parekh

Puzzle Contributor: Tim Preston

Contents

Series Editor: Gaby Waters

Puzzle checkers: Harriet Castor and Christina Hopkinson

You will need a pencil, an eraser and some sheets of tracing paper to tackle the puzzles on the pages ahead.

Before You Start

Treasure charts, classic labyrinths, old plans, coded maps ... all these and more lie in wait on the pages ahead. Some of the puzzles are moderately tricky, while others could prove fiendishly difficult. But watch out – it may not be obvious which are which.

To solve the puzzles, look carefully at the illustrations and read the documents thoroughly. It won't be easy. Some of the diaries and letters may be written in strange scripts with odd spellings – but, once deciphered, they could contain vital information. Sometimes you may need to crack a code or figure out a brainteaser before you can even begin to find the answer.

Should you need any help – and you may – there are clues on page 42 to point you in the right direction. And if you are finally stumped, turn to pages 43-48 to find the answers with detailed explanations.

You can pick out a puzzle at random to solve, if you dare. But if you start at the beginning and tackle them in order, you will discover several stories emerging, with a recurring cast of characters. To make sense of these, read on ...

Zoonal Duo and the Mission to Save Quirk

Zoonal Duo is a two-headed troubleshooter from the Ninth Universe. In the space-year 9992 the rulers of the Planet Zarka are planning to transform the Ninth Universe into a giant labyrinth of spaceways. But one planet stands in their way – Quirk, the cradle of civilization. Zoonal's mission is to save Quirk from destruction and thus rescue the Ninth Universe from a labyrinthine fate. The contents of a time capsule which mysteriously appeared in Quirk's southern hemisphere chart Zoonal's journey across space . . . and time.

Hercula and the Five Mighty Feats

Hercula is the local heroine of Harmonika, an island off the coast of Mythika and the heart of one of Quirk's ancient civilizations. Thousands of years ago, the Mythikan Deities decreed that whoever could perform their five tricky tasks would win the Golden Ladle of Heroism. Hercula's bid for this ultimate prize is the subject of five frescoes, discovered by amateur archaeologist Milo Midnight on Harmonika a few years ago.

Sir Gelfrid and Hildegarde and the Singing Rock

Sir Gelfrid and his apprentice knight, Hildegarde, live in the beleaguered kingdom of Loen during Quirk's Dark Age of the Seven Kingdoms. The valiant duo are searching for the Singing Rock which, legend says, will restore joy to Loen. Their adventures are told using a series of illustrations from Dark Age manuscripts.

Waldo Widget and the Search for El Taco

Waldo Widget is a Twystian from the Golden Age of the Seven Kingdoms. He has been a courtier at the palace of Queen Pompadora but then dares to criticize her pet goose, Gosric. The furious queen promptly announces that Waldo is banished from Twystia for life unless he finds the legendary city of El Taco in the recently-discovered land of Terra Nova and sails back with ship-loads of gold. Waldo's travels are illustrated with maps and ancient diaries, now in the museums of Tukan and of Twystia City.

Agent Mistral and the Elite Gang

Four hundred years later, during the Great Gang Era, Terra Nova's Secret Service sends Waldo's descendant, Agent Mistral, to Twystia. Her mission is to investigate the sinister activities of the Elite Gang and its leader, Lucasta Bombasta. Details of this top-secret operation have been pieced together using Mistral's maps and papers, until recently locked in the vaults of the Secret Service HQ.

The Quest

There's more to these five tales than meets the eye, for lying hidden in their midst is a strange story of a stone with legendary powers, now lost in the mists of time. If you keep your eyes open, you can unravel its tangled history. But remember, as centuries pass, it is not only names that can change their form. On page 48, there are hints to lead you on the trail of the stone. But the solution to the central mystery – the location of the lost stone – lies elsewhere in the book for you to find.

The Ancient Star Chart

The Zarkans are preparing to destroy the Planet Quirk in the first phase of their masterplan to build the giant labyrinth of spaceways across the Ninth Universe. The Zarkans' weapon of destruction is the D Ray which can only be neutralized by the Crystal of Leyheyhey. This magical crystal is hidden on one of the 35 stars of the constellation known as the Warp of Arg. In his bid to save Quirk, alien adventurer Zoonal Duo must find the crystal by searching every star in the Warp. But first he has to plot a course along its starways using this ancient star chart.

What is Zoonal's route?

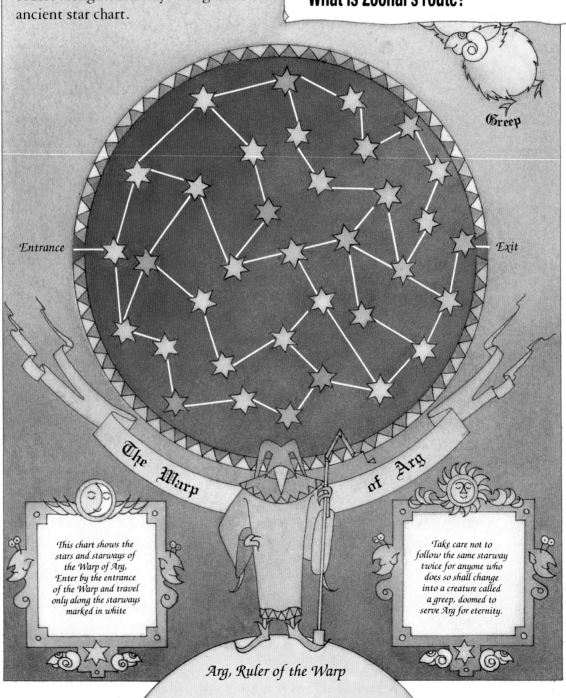

Greep

Entrance

Exit

The Warp of Arg

This chart shows the stars and starways of the Warp of Arg. Enter by the entrance of the Warp and travel only along the starways marked in white

Take care not to follow the same starway twice for anyone who does so shall change into a creature called a greep, doomed to serve Arg for eternity.

Arg, Ruler of the Warp

The Labyrinth of Ouzo

For the first of her five feats, Harmonika's local heroine Hercula must free Thrumos, musician to the god Malinger, from the Labyrinth of Ouzo the three-headed satyr. For five long months, Thrumos has been forced to play melodies to soothe Ouzo's triple monster headache, caused by eating the Giant Chocolate Cake of the goddess Migraine. Hercula has Malinger's plan of the labyrinth, depicted on this Harmonikan fresco, to help her find the way. Each matching pair of dots marks the entrance and exit of one of Ouzo's five secret tunnels which run between different sections of his maze. The tunnels themselves are not shown on the plan.

OUZO AND THRUMOS

What is Hercula's route?

5

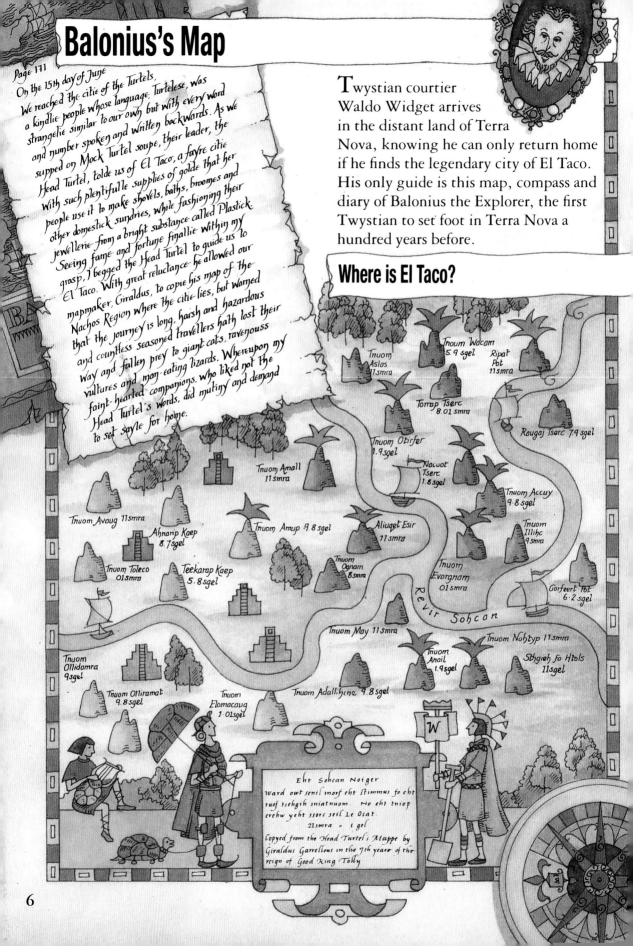

Balonius's Map

Page 171

On the 15th day of June

We reached the citie of the Turtels, a kindlie people whose language, Turtelese, was strangelie similar to our own but with every word and number spoken and written backwards. As we supped on Mock Turtel soupe, their leader, the Head Turtel, tolde us of El Taco, a fayre citie with such plentifulle supplies of golde that her people use it to make shovels, baths, broomes and other domestick sundries, while fashioning their jewellerie from a bright substance called Plastick. Seeing fame and fortune finallie within my grasp, I begged the Head Turtel to guide us to El Taco. With great reluctance he allowed our mapmaker, Giraldus, to copie his map of the Nachos Region where the citie lies, but warned that the journey is long, harsh and hazardous and countless seasoned travellers hath lost their way and fallen prey to giant cats, ravenouss vultures and man-eating lizards. Whereupon my faint-hearted companions, who liked not the Head Turtel's words, did mutiny and demand to set sayle for home.

T wystian courtier Waldo Widget arrives in the distant land of Terra Nova, knowing he can only return home if he finds the legendary city of El Taco. His only guide is this map, compass and diary of Balonius the Explorer, the first Twystian to set foot in Terra Nova a hundred years before.

Where is El Taco?

Tnuom Aslas 11smra

Tnuom Wacam 5.9 sgel

Ripat Pot 11smra

Torrap Tserc 8.01 smra

Rougaj Tserc 7.9 sgel

Tnuom Otirfer 1.9 sgel

Nacuot Tserc 1.8 sgel

Tnuom Accuy 9.8 sgel

Tnuom Amall 11smra

Tnuom Amup 9.8 sgel

Aliuqet Esir 11smra

Tnuom Illihc 9 smra

Tnuom Avaug 11smra

Ahnarip Kaep 8.7 sgel

Teekarap Kaep 5.8 sgel

Tnuom Ognam 8smra

Tnuom Evorgnam 01smra

Gorfeert Pot 6.2 sgel

Tnuom Toleco 01smra

Revir Sohcan

Tnuom May 11smra

Tnuom Nohtyp 11smra

Tnuom Anail 1.9sgel

Sthgieh fo Htols 11sgel

Tnuom Ollidomra 9 sgel

Tnuom Olliramat 9.8 sgel

Tnuom Elomacauq 1.01gel

Tnuom Adallihene 9.8 sgel

W

Eht Sohcan Noiger
Ward owt senil morf eht stimmus fo eht ruof tsehgih sniatnuom. No eht tniop erehw yeht ssorc seil Le Ocat.
21smra = 1 gel
Copied from the Head Turtel's Mappe by Giraldus Garrelons in the 7th yeare of the reign of Good King Tolly

Mappa Blundi

Sir Gelfrid and his apprentice knight, Hildegarde, ride out from the land of Loen in search of the Singing Rock of Lollo Rosso. Unfortunately neither of them know where Lollo Rosso is. By chance they reach the city of Twystia, home of the Mappa Blundi. This famous map depicts all seven cities of the seven kingdoms of the Dark Age world, but the duo must unravel the cryptic clues below the map to discover which city is which.

Citie

Citie

Citie

Citie

Citie

Citie

Citie

Twystia Citie lyes due west of Crocodopolis Citie

Groen Citie lyes north-west of Crocodopolis Citie

Mythika Citie lyes due east of Desperanda Citie

Each Citie shares the name of its Kingdom

Due south-east of Loen Citie lyes the Citie of Lollo Rosso

Which is the city of Lollo Rosso?

The Metro Map

Dispatched to the distant land of Twystia to investigate the shady activities of the Elite Gang, Terra Novan secret agent Mistral has to make contact with a fellow agent at a station on Twystia City's metro system. All the bewildered agent has to go on is a cryptic telegram, found inside a brown envelope from HQ together with a metro map, a ticket, a newspaper clipping and two photographs.

Where is Mistral's rendezvous?

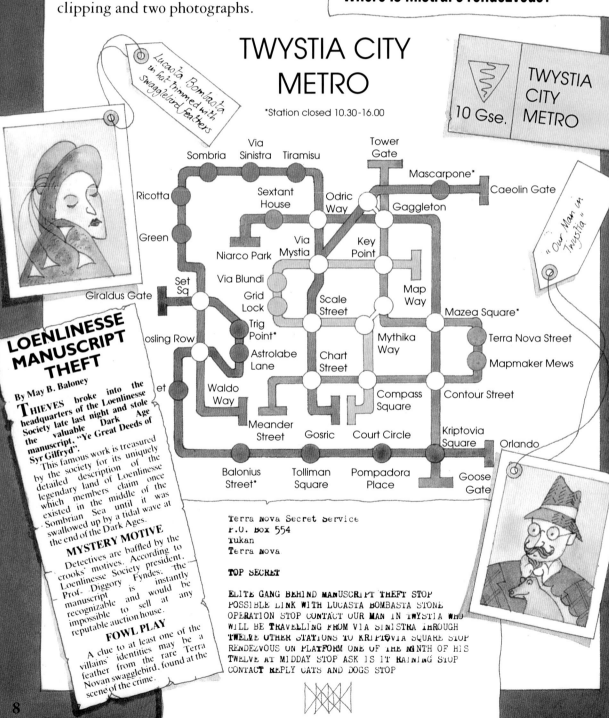

TWYSTIA CITY METRO

*Station closed 10.30–16.00

TWYSTIA CITY METRO

10 Gse.

Lucasta Bombasta in hat trimmed with swagglebird feathers

"Our Man in Twystia"

Stations shown on map: Via Sombria, Via Sinistra, Tiramisu, Tower Gate, Mascarpone*, Caeolin Gate, Ricotta, Sextant House, Odric Way, Gaggleton, Green, Via Mystia, Key Point, Niarco Park, Set Sq, Via Blundi, Scale Street, Map Way, Mazea Square*, Giraldus Gate, Grid Lock, Terra Nova Street, Trig Point*, Astrolabe Lane, Chart Street, Mythika Way, Mapmaker Mews, Gosling Row, Waldo Way, Compass Square, Contour Street, Meander Street, Gosric, Court Circle, Kriptovia Square, Orlando, Balonius Street*, Tolliman Square, Pompadora Place, Goose Gate

LOENLINESSE MANUSCRIPT THEFT

By May B. Baloney

THIEVES broke into the headquarters of the Loenlinesse Society late last night and stole the valuable Dark Age manuscript, "Ye Great Deeds of Syr Gilfryd".

This famous work is treasured by the society for its uniquely detailed description of the legendary land of Loenlinesse which members claim once existed in the middle of the Sombrian Sea until it was swallowed up by a tidal wave at the end of the Dark Ages.

MYSTERY MOTIVE

Detectives are baffled by the crooks' motives. According to Loenlinesse Society president, Prof. Diggory Fyndes, the manuscript is instantly recognizable and would be impossible to sell at any reputable auction house.

FOWL PLAY

A clue to at least one of the villains' identities may be a feather from the rare Terra Novan swagglebird, found at the scene of the crime.

Terra Nova Secret Service
P.O. Box 554
Tukan
Terra Nova

TOP SECRET

ELITE GANG BEHIND MANUSCRIPT THEFT STOP
POSSIBLE LINK WITH LUCASTA BOMBASTA STONE
OPERATION STOP CONTACT OUR MAN IN TWYSTIA WHO
WILL BE TRAVELLING FROM VIA SINISTRA THROUGH
TWELVE OTHER STATIONS TO KRIPTOVIA SQUARE STOP
RENDEZVOUS ON PLATFORM ONE OF THE NINTH OF HIS
TWELVE AT MIDDAY STOP ASK IS IT RAINING STOP
CONTACT REPLY CATS AND DOGS STOP

The Deadly Dance

For her second feat, Hercula must retrieve the bouzouki of the god Karioki from the Dolmadean Dogbeasts by performing their Deadly Dance with her partner, Thrumos. This Harmonikan fresco shows the dancefloor, a great eight-pointed star, with the dancers in their starting positions. There is a total of seven moves in the dance. When it ends, all the dancers must have switched positions with the person diagonally opposite them. In a single move, each dancer twirls along the white marble way that leads straight to the next point and may go on to other points, as long as no other dancers lurk there. Hercula has to make the first move — one wrong step and the Dogbeasts will rip their rivals limb from limb.

What are the seven moves of the dance?

Orlando Bombasto's Map

In Tukan, Terra Nova's capital city, no one has heard of El Taco or the Nachos Region. The people of Tukan offer to guide Waldo Widget to the map-making town of Triangula, deep in the Terra Novan jungle. But first Waldo must find the city's lost magic charm, the Turquoise Amulet of Twitta. During his search, Waldo stumbles upon a Twystian plan of the Great Square of Tukan, together with a locket and a coded message addressed to Orlando Bombasto, a shady fellow adventurer staying in the city.

Where is the amulet?

fishpond

statue

statue

fishpond

fishpond

Orlando
Uif Uvsrvpjtf Bnvmfu
pg Uxjuub jt cvsjfe
voefs uif ufff evf tpvui
pg uif qmbdf xifsf uif
opsuifsonptu pg uif
tjy tubuvft podt tuppe

Marco Niarco

W°

A Plan of the Great Square of Tukan
In this square there once stood six golden statues of the six toucans who led Twitta, founder of Tukan, to the city's site. As the toucans were held to be of equal merit, no statue was placed in vertical, horizontal or diagonal line with any other lest it be cast into shadow by its follows. Legend says that ere Balonius's shippe was sighted offshore, four statues took flight.

A Hiking Map

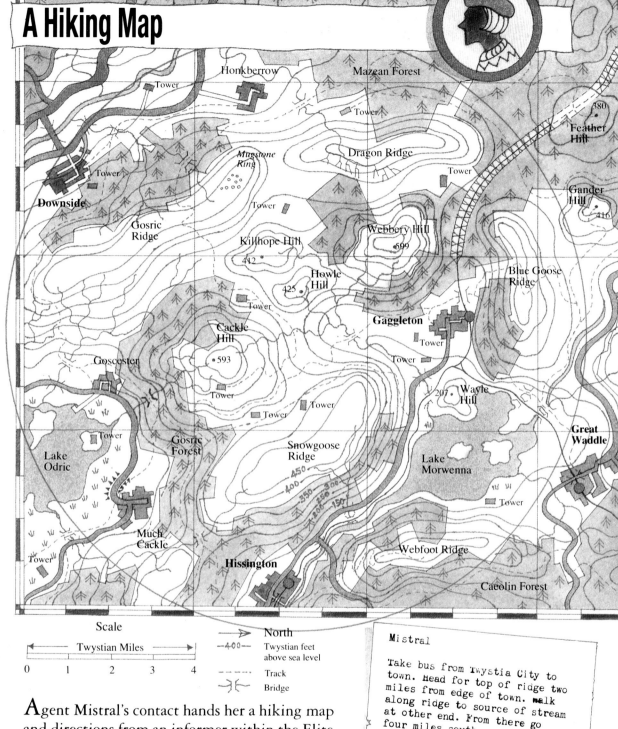

Honkberrow

Mazean Forest

Tower

Tower

380

Feather Hill

Dragon Ridge

Mugstone Ring

Tower

Tower

Gander Hill

416

Downside

Tower

Gosric Ridge

Tower

Killhope Hill

Webbery Hill

599

412

Howle Hill

425

Blue Goose Ridge

Cackle Hill

Gaggleton

Tower

Goscester

593

Tower

Tower

207 Wayle Hill

Tower

Tower

Tower

Great Waddle

Lake Odric

Gosric Forest

Snowgoose Ridge

Lake Morwenna

450
400
350 300
200 250 150

Tower

Much Cackle

Tower

Webfoot Ridge

Hissington

Caeolin Forest

Scale

→ North

Twystian Miles

−400− Twystian feet above sea level

0   1   2   3   4

------- Track

⊣⊢ Bridge

Agent Mistral's contact hands her a hiking map and directions from an informer within the Elite Gang, codenamed Cyclone. Cyclone has left a package of vital information in a ruined tower in the Twystian countryside. Mistral must collect it without delay.

What is Mistral's route?

Mistral

Take bus from Twystia City to town. Head for top of ridge two miles from edge of town. Walk along ridge to source of stream at other end. From there go four miles south-west then turn north-west and continue cross-country until you reach track. Follow track to bridge. Tower lies halfway between bridge and top of highest hill. Package is in chest by doorway.

Cyclone

NB Directions apply to area ringed in red.

The Pyramid Maze

For her third feat Hercula must retrieve the Crocodile Crown of Crocodopola, the goddess of Crocodopolis. This fabulous crown was stolen by Papyrut the magpie god and hidden in one of the chambers of the Pyramid of Ar. To find the crown, Hercula must follow a secret trail of symbols through the pyramid, guided by the cryptic contents of the scrolls of Ar. A translation of the scrolls appears on this unusual Harmonikan fresco, together with a cut-away view of the pyramid, drawn in the quirky style of Ancient Crocodopolis.

SCROLL OF AR

A TRAIL OF THREE SYMBOLS LEADS TO THE CROCODILE CROWN. ONE OR MORE OF THESE SYMBOLS APPEAR IN EACH ROOM TOGETHER WITH FALSE SYMBOLS. ENTER THE PYRAMID AND LOOK FOR THE 1ST SYMBOL IN THE 1ST ROOM, THE 2ND IN THE 2ND, THE 3RD IN THE 3RD, THEN THE 1ST IN THE 4TH, THE 2ND IN THE 5TH AND THE 3RD IN THE 6TH. CONTINUE TO FOLLOW THE TRAIL UNTIL YOU FIND THE 3RD IN THE 36TH. IN THIS ROOM YOU WILL FIND THE CROWN. BUT BEWARE — THE CURSE OF AR SHALL FALL ON ANY WHO ENTER THE SAME ROOM TWICE

SCROLL OF AR

THIS ROW OF SYMBOLS CONTAINS ONE OF THE THREE SECRET SYMBOLS BUT IT IS NOT IN ITS RIGHT ORDER IN THE SEQUENCE

THIS ROW OF SYMBOLS CONTAINS ONE OF THE THREE SECRET SYMBOLS AND IT IS IN ITS RIGHT ORDER IN THE SEQUENCE

Where is the Crocodile Crown?

A Plan of Fortress Howles

On the way to Lollo Rosso, a sinister stranger, the Long Knight of Howles, invites Sir Gelfrid and Hildegarde to supper at his fortress. As soon as the duo enter the castle, their host locks them in a tiny turret cell to feed to Brimstone, his greedy pet dragon for breakfast the next day. Before they can despair, a swagglebird taps on the window. It brings a plan and a picture of the fortress, together with a skeleton key, from the great enchanter, Vaeralyn.

Sirs Odric, Caedin and Guinevere
Languish in this dungeon dreare

Knights

of the

Blue Goose

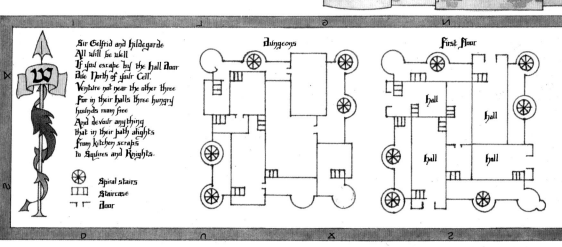

Sir Gelfrid and Hildegarde
All will be well
If you escape by the hall door
Due North of your Cell.
Venture not near the other three
For in their halls three hungry
hounds roam free
And devour anything
that in their path alights
from kitchen scraps
to Squires and Knights.

⊛ Spiral stairs
▥ Staircase
⊓ Door

Dungeons

First Floor

hall

hall

hall

hall

With the aid of these gifts, Gelfrid and Hildegarde plan their escape. On their way, they must rescue three other prisoners, the Knights of the Blue Goose, from the Long Knight's deepest, darkest dungeon. But they must also avoid the savage Dolmadean hounds who keep watch in three of the fortress's four great halls while the Long Knight and Brimstone sleep.

This key will undo every lock and door of any palace, fortress or tower.

Sir Gelfrid
and
hildegarde

In this cell
Lock'd and barr'd
Lye Sir Gelfrid
And hildegarde.

What is their route?

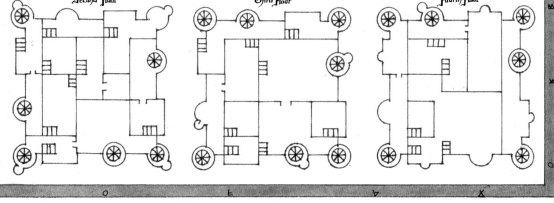

Second Floor

Third Floor

Fourth Floor

The Triangulan Chart

Accompanied by Orlando Bombasto and a Tukan guide, Waldo Widget reaches the town of Triangula. But the people have never heard of El Taco and seem puzzled by Balonius's map. After much debate, Waldo decides to find the Turtels who told Balonius about El Taco. The Triangulans give Waldo this map of the Terra Novan jungle to guide him, but he must turn to Balonius's diary to decipher their directions before he can work out his route.

What is Waldo's route to the Turtels?

Triangulan description of location of city of Turtels on map opposite. Map also shows location of Triangula.

Page 11

On our arrival the Triangulans looked at our caps and gowns with mirth and cryed "Why are ye so square?" for these meme folk are most triangular in dresse. While we feasted in the Great Triangula Hall, a worthy sage proclaimed that the latest Twystian theory that the world is shaped lyke a ball is wrong and that it is really pyramid shaped. He went on to explain how the Triangulans have subdivided the world into a grid of triangles. If a traveller seeks directions to a citie, the Triangulans list the corners of the triangle in which the citie is located, then the traveller follows a straight line between Triangula and his or her destination. The following sketch is a copie of the Triangulans' description of their own citie's location, written in their strange script with a translation below.

Triangula lyes in the triangle at the place where the toucan sings. The corners of the triangle are the stone of the jaguar, the temple of the sloth and the temple of the snake goddesse.

Page 12

How many folk have lost their way following Triangulan directions I know not.

Balonius   Triangulan

16

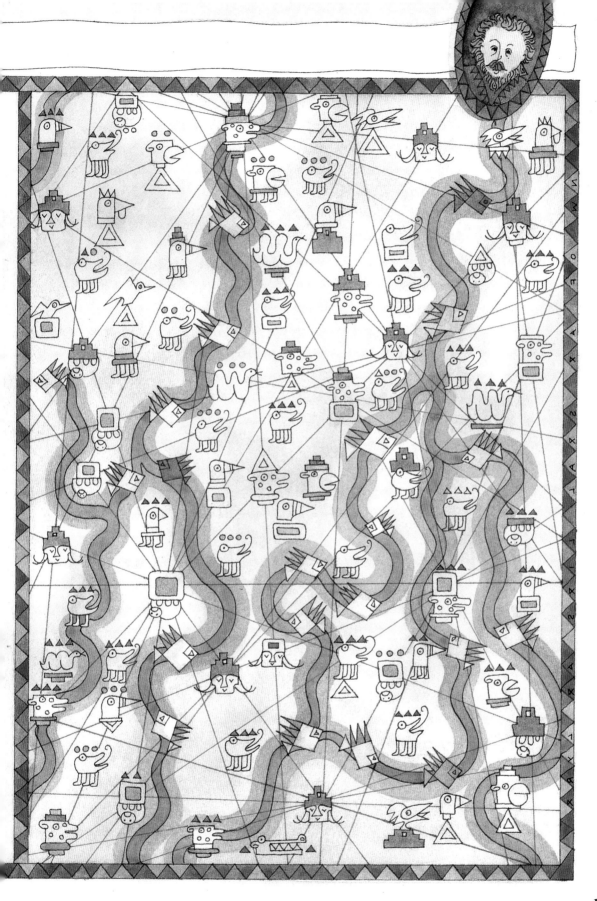

The Two Maps of Zarka City

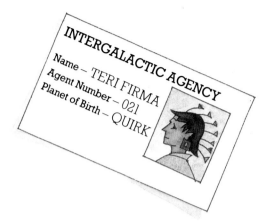

INTERGALACTIC AGENCY
Name – TERI FIRMA
Agent Number – 021
Planet of Birth – QUIRK

INTERGALACTIC INTELLIGENCE FILE
Name – GYGYDDION
Agent Number – 002
Planet of birth – GIDDIO
Mission – to enter Zarka City and search for details of secret Zarkan masterplan.

Outcome – Vital documents seized and despatched to HQ. 002 captured by Zarkan agents and taken to Labyrinka Prison.
Observations – Prison unguarded in belief that would-be rescuers will lose way in Zarka City's notorious one-way system.
Maps show: 1/ main roads
2/ enlargement of grid square (E3) where prison is located with minor roads added. X marks prison.
Intergalactic Skeleton Key will unlock all doors.

Now Zoonal Duo has found the Crystal of Leyheyhey, his next task is to cross the Time Warp and bring it to the Planet Quirk. This may prove to be the most dangerous and difficult part of his mission, for in the entire history of space exploration, only one spaceship, under the command of Gidius of the Planet Giddio, has ever made a successful landing on the doomed planet. It was reported that Gidius passed on the secret of his landing approach route to his great-grandson, Gygyddion, an agent for the Intergalactic Agency. Unfortunately Gygyddion was captured by the Zarkans during an undercover operation in Zarka City and he is now a prisoner in the Labyrinka Prison. Accompanied by Teri Firma, an explorer from Quirk now working for the Agency, Zoonal must rescue Gygyddion, using two maps of Zarka City and the contents of an Intergalactic Intelligence File.

What is Zoonal's route to the prison?

THE DECLARATION OF THE MAZE-MAKERS OF ZARKA

In the beginning, our ancestors on Quirk learned how to devise mazes. These proved to be so simple that even the most foolish of the Quirkans would eventually find the secret route.

Under our stewardship, the maze is about to reach its true destiny. By building the giant labyrinth of spaceways, Zarkan power will extend into every corner of the Ninth Universe. No one but the Zarkans will know the way between each planet, star, comet and galaxy. All who oppose us shall be sent to wander the endless loops of the giant labyrinth for eternity.

First we must remove the Planet Quirk from the path of the first spaceway. On the Quirkan day 01012100, the Great D Ray shall strike the planet at grid reference 768557. With Quirk's destruction, we shall herald the dawn of the New Era of the Planet Zarka.

18

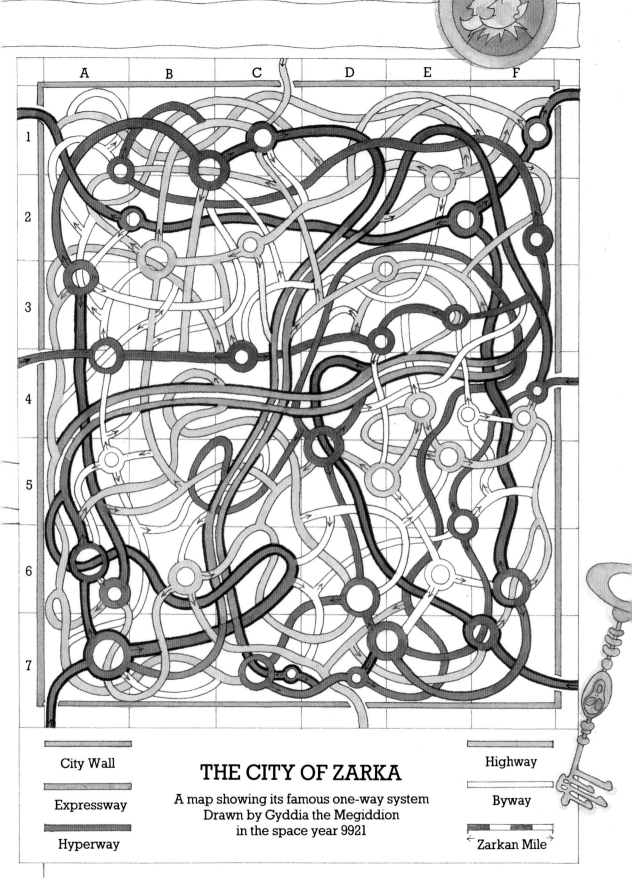

THE CITY OF ZARKA

A map showing its famous one-way system
Drawn by Gyddia the Megiddion
in the space year 9921

City Wall

Expressway

Hyperway

Highway

Byway

← Zarkan Mile →

A Plan of the Casa Fantasa

Acting on the contents of Cyclone's package, Agent Mistral prepares to enter the Casa Fantasa, the ritzy seaside retreat of the Elite Gang's leader, Lucasta Bombasta, in the land of Mascarpone. Mistral has only five minutes to find a mysterious parcel, believed to contain the stolen Mappa Blundi, and leave before the house's alarm system is activated.

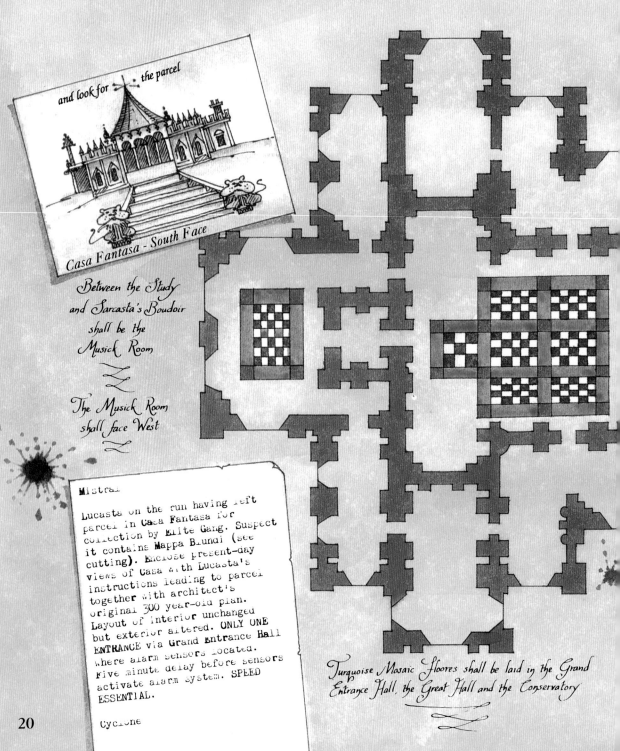

and look for the parcel

Casa Fantasa - South Face

Between the Study
and Sarcasta's Boudoir
shall be the
Musick Room

The Musick Room
shall face West

Mistral

Lucasta on the run having left
parcel in Casa Fantasa for
collection by Elite Gang. Suspect
it contains Mappa Blundi (see
cutting). Enclose present-day
views of Casa with Lucasta's
instructions leading to parcel
together with architect's
original 300 year-old plan.
Layout of interior unchanged
but exterior altered. ONLY ONE
ENTRANCE via Grand Entrance Hall
where alarm sensors located.
Five minute delay before sensors
activate alarm system. SPEED
ESSENTIAL.

Cyclone

Turquoise Mosaic Floores shall be laid in the Grand
Entrance Hall, the Great Hall and the Conservatory

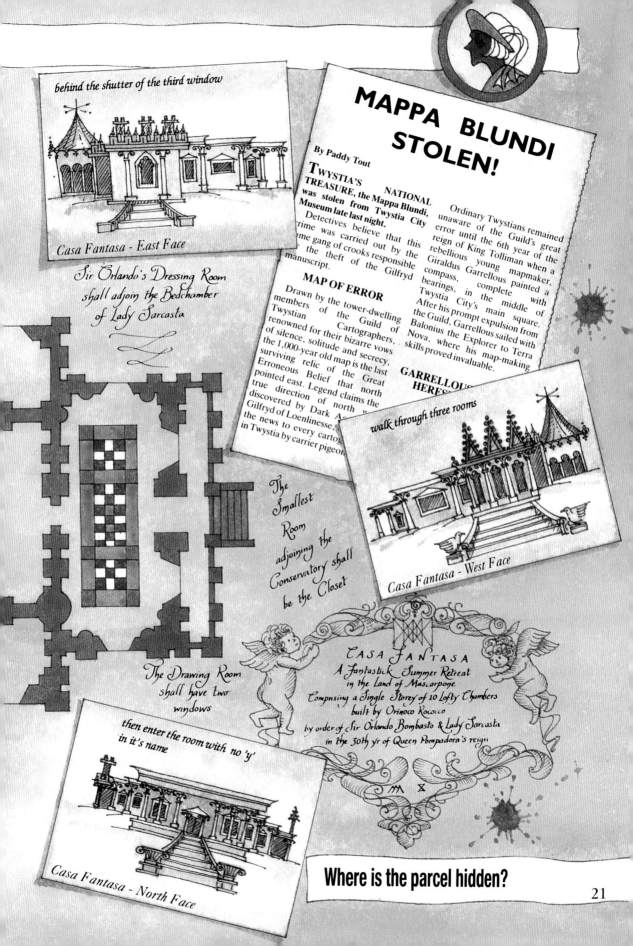

behind the shutter of the third window

Casa Fantasa - East Face

*Sir Orlando's Dressing Room
shall adjoin the Bedchamber
of Lady Sarcasta*

MAPPA BLUNDI STOLEN!

By Paddy Tout

TWYSTIA'S NATIONAL TREASURE, the Mappa Blundi, was stolen from Twystia City Museum late last night.

Detectives believe that this crime was carried out by the same gang of crooks responsible for the theft of the Gilfryd manuscript.

MAP OF ERROR

Drawn by the tower-dwelling members of the Guild of Twystian Cartographers, renowned for their bizarre vows of silence, solitude and secrecy, the 1,000-year old map is the last surviving relic of the Great Erroneous Belief that north pointed east. Legend claims the true direction of north was discovered by Dark A... Gilfryd of Loenlinesse, ... the news to every cartog... in Twystia by carrier pigeon...

Ordinary Twystians remained unaware of the Guild's great error until the 6th year of the reign of King Tolliman when a rebellious young mapmaker, Giraldus Garrellous painted a compass, complete with bearings, in the middle of Twystia City's main square. After his prompt expulsion from the Guild, Garrellous sailed with Balonius the Explorer to Terra Nova, where his map-making skills proved invaluable.

GARRELLOU... HERES...

walk through three rooms

Casa Fantasa - West Face

The Smallest Room adjoining the Conservatory shall be the Closet

*CASA FANTASA
A Fantastick Summer Retreat
in the Land of Mascarpone
Comprising a Single Storey of 10 Lofty Chambers
built by Orinoco Rococo
by order of Sir Orlando Bombasto & Lady Sarcasta
in the 30th yr of Queen Pompadora's reign*

*The Drawing Room
shall have two
windows*

then enter the room with no 'y'
in it's name

Casa Fantasa - North Face

Where is the parcel hidden?

The Labyrinth of Amphibia

THRVMOS AND HERCVLA

For her fourth feat, Hercula must bring the Magic Blancmange of Baklava to Semolino, the youngest of the Five Princes of Twystia. The goddess Amphibia imprisoned the five princes in her labyrinth, depicted on this Harmonikan fresco, and decreed that each would turn into a frog on their 8th birthday, as a punishment for stealing her five sacred tadpoles. The spell will be broken if

SEMOLINO AND HIS BROTHERS

Semolino eats the Magic Blancmange before his 8th birthday. Unfortunately Hercula has only five minutes to find her way through the labyrinth and reach him before it is too late.

What is Hercula's route?

A Map of Lollo Rosso

At last Sir Gelfrid and Hildegarde reach the kingdom of Lollo Rosso with 20 Twystian geese and a bag of gold, a reward from the three Knights of the Blue Goose. They are disguised as goose traders, for Bombastus the evil ruler of Lollo Rosso has decreed that only geese and their owners are allowed into his realm. Using this goose trader's map, Gelfrid and Hildegarde must decide which of Lollo Rosso's four gates to enter before they make their way through a maze of towns and tollgates to Bombastus's Castle where the Singing Rock lies hidden.

A Mappe of Lollo Rosso
for Goose Traders + their Ilk

Numbers in Green Flags show
the exact number of geese allowed
through each gate into Lollo Rosso
Surplus geese may be left with the gatekeepers

Numbers in White Flags show
how many geese may be purchased
at this citie or town

Numbers in Red Flags show how many
geese must be given in payment to the keeper
of each tollhouse or ferry

What is their route?

A Map of Bokonsrikta

On his way to the Turtel people, Waldo Widget is captured by snake charmers from Bokonsrikta. They take Waldo back to their city and lock him in the Temple of Pythonia, the snake goddess, to juggle with ten venomous snakes in the 20th Pythonic Games the next day. Waldo turns to Balonius's diary, only to discover that his bag has been switched. The bag in its place contains a length of bright material, a locket, a letter, a page from a diary, a Twystian map of Bokonsrikta and a key. Although these items won't help Waldo with his snake juggling, they will help him escape from the city.

What is Waldo's safest escape route?

Friday

Ditermined to have Golden Idle for fowntain at Chateau Niarco, I sett off for Grate Temple of Pythonia on morn of Bokonsrikta's 15th Pythonic Games. As customerrie during Games, citie desserted except for 3 gards keeping watch frum 3 towers. Guards had good view down streetes radiating frum areas around their towers, but that was all they coulde see, for their towers are not veri tall. I kept to backstreetes and courtyardes, except for 11 occasions when I hadde to rush across streetes within view of towers. Luckilie I coulde see when guards turned their heads before I made my moove. At last I reached a dustie courtyard surrounded by houses on 3½ sides. In middle stude Grate Temple of Pythonia – a huge stepped pyramidd with 2 redde stones on its summit. I

To my most worthless son Orlando

Repair your low position in my esteem by fynding the Stone of Bombastus that was yielded unto our renowned ancestor by vanquished Harmonikans at the dawn of the great Dark Age, then mysteriouslie loste. A clue to its fate may lye in this fragment of material. A picture on its border shows the Stone in the handes of two Strangelie-costumed folke. As my olde friend Marco Niarco found the fragment in Bokonsrikta, I fancy that this Terra Novan citie may holde the secret of the Stone's hiding place. Therefore I urge you to hasten to Bokonsrikta and search every temple and dwelling with the aid of this skeleton key and mappe which Marco hath kindlie lent us, together with a page from his journal.

On your way to Bokonsrikta forget not to collect the Turquoise Amulet of Twitta from the citie of Tukan. Before he set off for Bokonsrikta, Marco took the amulet and hid it somewhere safe. So thrilled was he with his Bokonsriktan booty that he forgot to retrieve the amulet before sailing home to Twystia.

Your loving mother

Agrippina

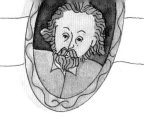

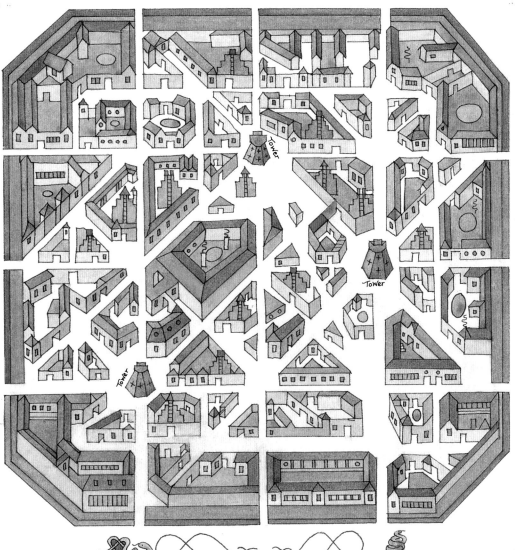

Tower

Tower

Tower

THE CITIE OF BOKONSRIKTA
In the lande of Terra Nova

Showing its Streets, its temples
its dwelling houses, its three watch-
towers & its 12 city gates

Drawne for Marco Hiarco
Esq.

By the Guild of Twystian Cartographers
in the fifth yeare of the reign of Queen
Pompadora

The Treasure Chart of Gidius

From the gytower on the gshores of Gmegiddio walk ΣM to the griver and follow it to its gsovrce. From there tvrn GM and travel 50 glygs in that gydirection before heading dve M. When yov are dve G of the temple gydoor, make yovr gyway ΣM to the gybank of the second griver then go 75 glygs M and 50 glygs G. This will bring yov to the gspot in the gypastvres by the gmovntains where my gychest lies bvried.

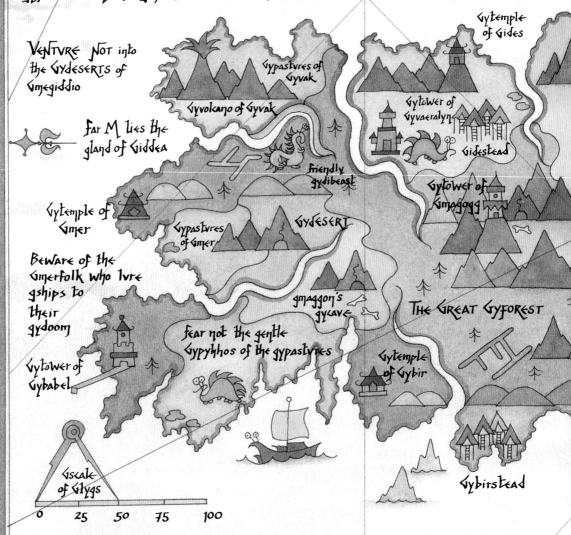

Ventvre Not into the Gydeserts of Gmegiddio

Far M lies the gland of Giddea

Gytemple of Gmer

Beware of the Gmerfolk who lvre gships to their gydoom

Gytower of Gybabel

Gypastvres of Gyvak

Gyvolkano of Gyvak

friendly gydibeast

Gypastvres of Gmer

Gydesert

fear not the gentle Gypykhos of the gypastvres

gmaggon's gycave

Gytemple of Gybir

Gytemple of Gides

Gytower of Gyvaeralyn

Gidestead

Gytower of Gmagogg

The Great Gyforest

Gybirstead

Gscale of Glygs

0   25   50   75   100

After Zoonal Duo and Teri Firma release Gygyddion from his Zarkan prison, he joins the mission to bring the Crystal of Leyheyhey to the Planet Quirk. But Gygyddion does not know the safe route to the surface of the doomed planet. The vital information was buried in a chest on the island of Megiddio on the Planet Giddio by his ancestor, Gidius, who led the only successful expedition to Quirk.

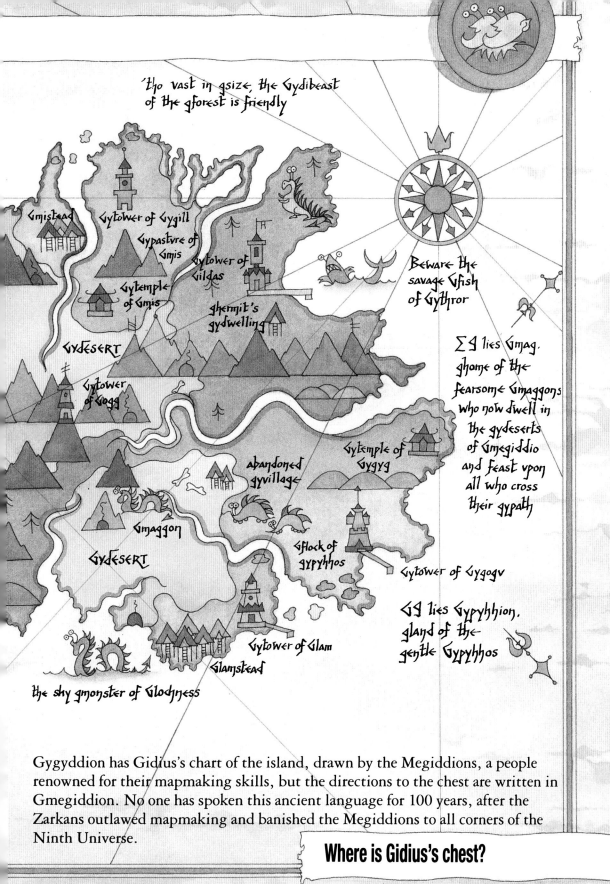

'tho vast in gsize, the Gydibeast of the gforest is friendly

Gmistead

Gytower of Gygill

Gypasture of Gmis

Gytower of Gildas

Gytemple of Gmis

ghennit's gydwelling

GYDESERT

Gytower of Gogg

Beware the savage Gfish of Gythror

∑ꟼ lies Gmag, ghome of the fearsome Gmaggons who now dwell in the gydeserts of Gmegiddio and feast upon all who cross their gypath

Gytemple of Gygyg

abandoned gyvillage

Gmaggon

GYDESERT

Gflock of Gypyhhos

Gytower of Gygogv

ꟼꟼ lies Gypyhhion, gland of the gentle Gypyhhos

Gytower of Glam

Glamstead

the shy gmonster of Glodhness

Gygyddion has Gidius's chart of the island, drawn by the Megiddions, a people renowned for their mapmaking skills, but the directions to the chest are written in Gmegiddion. No one has spoken this ancient language for 100 years, after the Zarkans outlawed mapmaking and banished the Megiddions to all corners of the Ninth Universe.

Where is Gidius's chest?

The Flight Chart

Inside the Casa Fantasa, Agent Mistral finds a parcel containing a letter from the Elite Gang's elusive leader, Lucasta Bombasta, and six envelopes addressed to her six fellow gang members. Inside each envelope is a set of six airline tickets leading to Lucasta's secret location. As a result of her complex itinerary, cunningly designed to throw detectives off her trail, the gangsters' journey will take three days. With the aid of a flight chart, can Agent Mistral find a swifter route to the crooks' mystery destination?

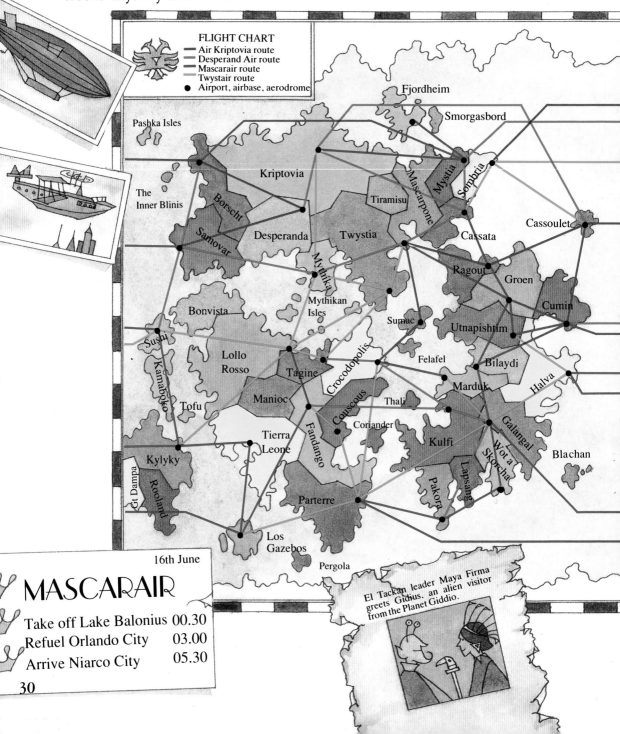

FLIGHT CHART
— Air Kriptovia route
— Desperand Air route
— Mascarair route
— Twystair route
● Airport, airbase, aerodrome

16th June

MASCARAIR

Take off Lake Balonius	00.30
Refuel Orlando City	03.00
Arrive Niarco City	05.30

El Tackan leader Maya Firma greets Gidius, an alien visitor from the Planet Giddio.

Desperand Air
16th/17th June

Take off Hercula Falls	21.15
Refuel Brimstone Basin	00.15
Arrive Rococco Airbase	01.15

TWYSTAIR
15th June

Take off Ricotta	17.30
Refuel Gosric	18.50
Refuel Gelfriston	21.45
Arrive Lake Balonius	23.50

14th June

Apologies for my sudden disappearance. The Twystian police are on my trail after they found a swagglebird feather from my hat in the Loenlinesse Society's HQ. Luckily our mission is almost at an end and soon the Stone of Bombastus will be in my hands. I have left sets of six air tickets for each of you. With these you must board the airship at Ricotta Aerodrome in Mascarpone disguised as Mythikan folk-dancers and lead detectives on a wild goose chase across the globe. When you reach your final destination, head for the harbour due south of the airfield, where I shall be waiting aboard my launch, The Lady Agrippina.

Lucasta

Map labels
- Edenland
- Zeroland
- Montaigna
- Old Cookey
- Spring County
- Spangleland
- New Maize
- Jalapeno
- Hacienda
- Ackee
- Daquiri
- Enchillada
- Iguana
- Terra Nova
- Chihuahua
- The Eastern Daubes
- Macaw
- Ewetopia
- Kylyky
- Great Dampa
- Llamalla
- The Sirocco Isles

Air Kriptobia
16th June

Take off Niarco City	10.30
Refuel Thrumos City	12.30
Refuel Blondi Airbase	14.40
Arrive Hudlum City	16.50

TWYSTAIR
17th June

| Take off Rococco Airbase | 04.45 |
| Arrive Port Vaeralyn | 06.00 |

MASCARAIR
16th June

Take off Hudlum City

Arrive Hercula Falls

What is Mistral's most direct route?

31

The Harmonikan Map

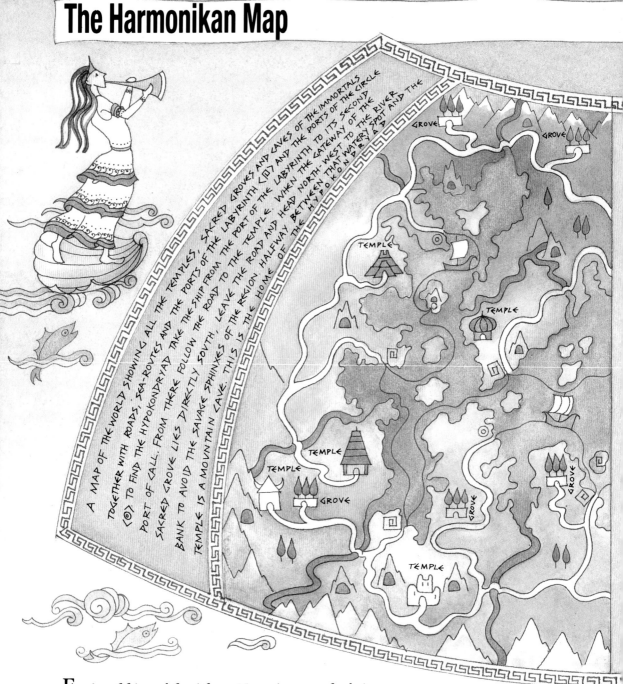

A MAP OF THE WORLD SHOWING ALL THE TEMPLES, SACRED GROVES AND CAVES OF THE IMMORTALS TOGETHER WITH ROADS, SEA-ROUTES AND THE PORTS OF THE LABYRINTH ⟨▣⟩ AND THE PORTS OF THE CIRCLE ⟨◉⟩ TO FIND THE HYPOKONDRYAD TAKE THE SHIP FROM THE PORT OF THE LABYRINTH TO ITS SECOND PORT OF CALL. FROM THERE FOLLOW THE ROAD TO THE TEMPLE. WHEN THE GATEWAY TO THE SACRED GROVE LIES DIRECTLY SOUTH, LEAVE THE ROAD AND HEAD NORTH-WEST TO THE RIVER BANK TO AVOID THE SAVAGE SPHINXES OF THE REGION. HALFWAY BETWEEN THAT WATERY SPOT AND THE TEMPLE IS A MOUNTAIN CAVE. THIS IS THE HOME OF THE HYPOKONDRYAD

GROVE

GROVE

TEMPLE

TEMPLE

TEMPLE

TEMPLE

GROVE

TEMPLE

GROVE

GROVE

TEMPLE

For her fifth and final feat, Hercula must find the Jewel of Joy. Long ago, Tikitaka, a sailor from a distant land presented this magical jewel to the gloomy Hypokondryad, the most beautiful of the immortals, after she announced that she would marry the mortal who could make her smile. Little did Tikitaka know that the Hypokondryad enjoyed being miserable so the Jewel of Joy just made sure that no one would ever succeed in making her smile.

Other suitors came, but their quest was doomed. Eventually they gave up and soon everyone forgot where the Hypokondryad lived or whether she existed. With the aid of the Mythikan Deities' map of the world, depicted on this Harmonikan fresco, can Hercula track down the Hypokondryad and the Jewel of Joy and win the Golden Ladle of Heroism?

Where is the Hypokondryad?

The Path Perilous

Still in disguise, Sir Gelfrid and Hildegarde step inside the Enchanted Hall of Bombastus's Castle. Across a checkered floor, diagonally opposite them, stands the Singing Rock, bathed in a mysterious blue light. Now they must find the invisible Path Perilous that leads to the magical rock and the end of their quest. But they must beware, for if they stray from the path, they will turn into wax figures. Their only guide is this strange painting of the castle from Vaeralyn the Enchanter. In the middle is the checkered floor, with the duo and the rock in their respective positions. Unlike the real floor, this painted floor is bordered with triangles, each bearing a number. Could these numbers, together with the small checkerboard on the right of the painting, hold the key to finding the Path Perilous?

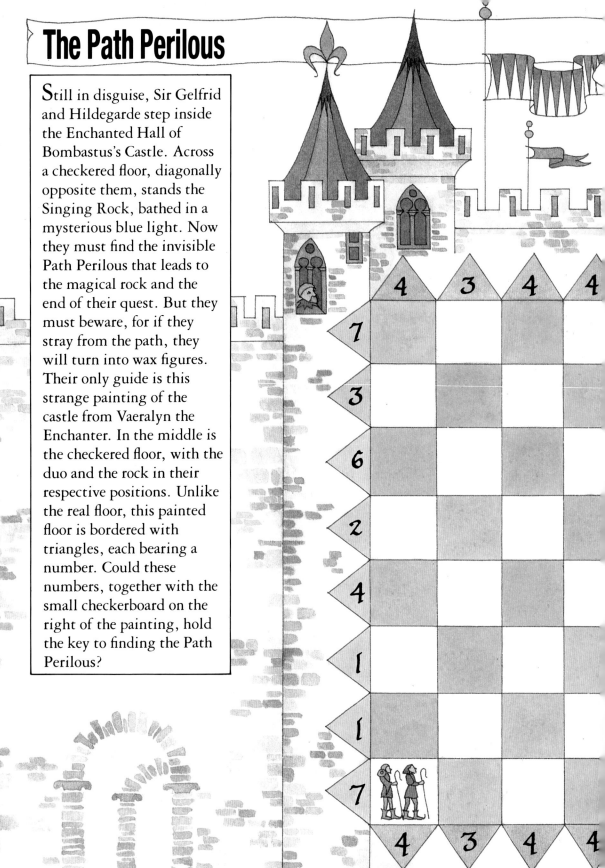

The Snake on this chequered board of aspect bizarre
Follows a route not seen by eye, the fabled Way of Ar.
Identical in principle yet harder in the test
Is that invisible Path Perilous you must tread to end your quest.

The numbers in the gold triangles display
How many squares in each row form part of the Way
While the numbers in the blue triangles show
Through how many squares in each column
the Way doth go.

Upwards, downwards and sideways the Way winds
But ne'er doth it travel in diagonal lines.

Where is the Path Perilous?

The Coded Carpet Map

Tuesday

Deeper into the jungle I ran, fearful lest the Bokonsriktans be on my trail, untill, close to exhaustion, I reached the smalle town of Chirpeecheep. Her people, the Cheeps, welcomed me with open arms on glimpsing my golden toucan Staff. This was my reward from the citizens of Tukan for fynding the amulet of Twitta, the founder of their city, who I learnt, was born in Chirpeecheep. To my delight, the Cheeps have heard of El Taco and will give me a mappe and directions when I have rested.

Tuesday evening

During a vast banquet, the Cheeps tolde me that El Taco lies exactly due ⊞⊡ of Chirpeecheep, due ⊞⊡ of Yucca, due ⊞⊡ of Tamarillo and due ⊡ of Guava. Seeing that I understood this not, the Cheeps' leader gave me one of his own compasses, with these strange directions writ thereon. Then his sonne presented me with a woven carpet. As I unrolled it, the leader explained that it was a mappe of the regions around El Taco and Chirpeecheep. According to him, the thick blue lines represent rivers, the thin red lines are roads,

the triangles like △ are mountains and volcanoes, and the large squares like ⊞ are townes and cities. Other large squares mark the entrances and exits of tunnels which are not shown on the mappe. Each tunnel links one road to another road and has its own symbol. To find out where a tunnel leads, the traveller must search for its matching symbol. Unlike the other symbols on the map, the tunnel symbols are sometimes upside-down or facing the left or right, so fynding a matching pair is a most difficult and perplexing task.

Wednesday morning

In preparation for my journey, I have donned comfortable El Tackan garb and given away my courtlie attire for I wish never to return to the petty intrigue of the Twystian court and end my days lavishing praise upon Queen

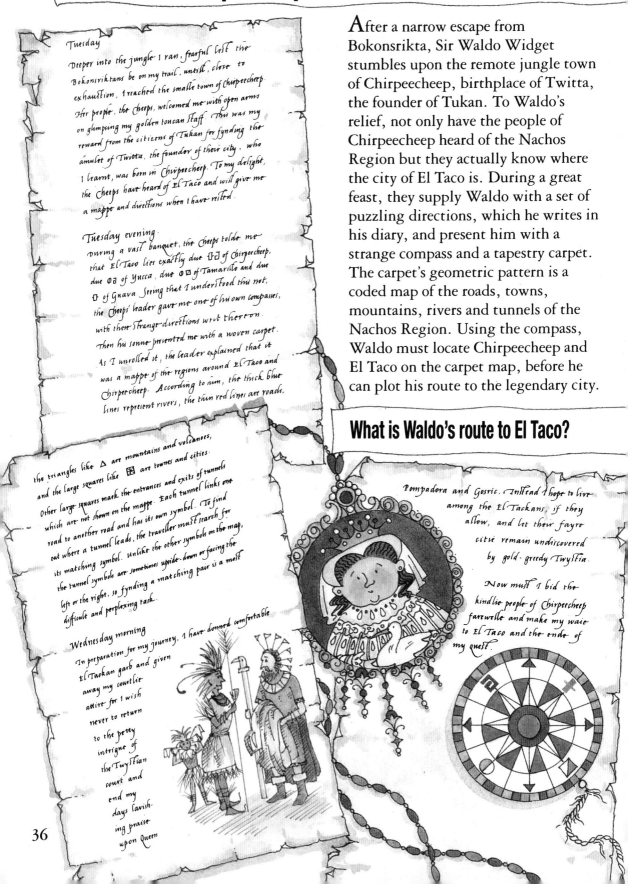

After a narrow escape from Bokonsrikta, Sir Waldo Widget stumbles upon the remote jungle town of Chirpeecheep, birthplace of Twitta, the founder of Tukan. To Waldo's relief, not only have the people of Chirpeecheep heard of the Nachos Region but they actually know where the city of El Taco is. During a great feast, they supply Waldo with a set of puzzling directions, which he writes in his diary, and present him with a strange compass and a tapestry carpet. The carpet's geometric pattern is a coded map of the roads, towns, mountains, rivers and tunnels of the Nachos Region. Using the compass, Waldo must locate Chirpeecheep and El Taco on the carpet map, before he can plot his route to the legendary city.

What is Waldo's route to El Taco?

Pompadora and Gosric. Instead I hope to live among the El Tackans, if they allow, and let their fayre citie remain undiscovered by gold-greedy Twystia.

Now must I bid the kindlie people of Chirpeecheep farewelle and make my waie to El Taco and the ende of my quest.

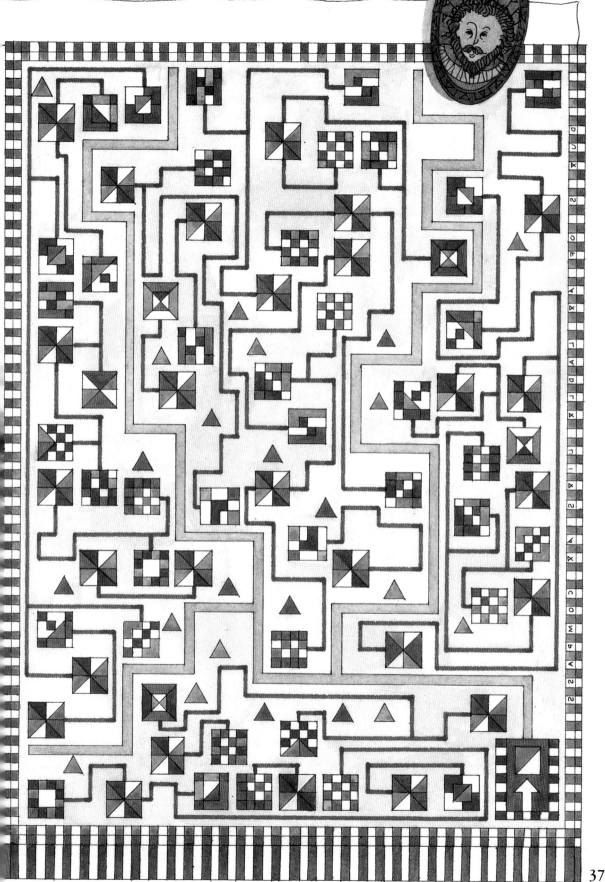

The Coded Map of Terra Nova

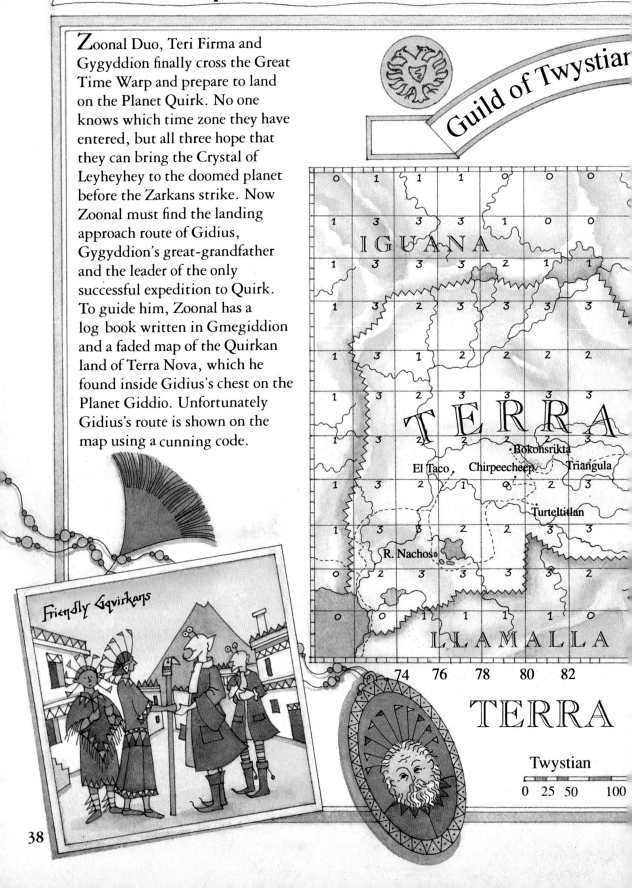

Zoonal Duo, Teri Firma and Gygyddion finally cross the Great Time Warp and prepare to land on the Planet Quirk. No one knows which time zone they have entered, but all three hope that they can bring the Crystal of Leyheyhey to the doomed planet before the Zarkans strike. Now Zoonal must find the landing approach route of Gidius, Gygyddion's great-grandfather and the leader of the only successful expedition to Quirk. To guide him, Zoonal has a log book written in Gmegiddion and a faded map of the Quirkan land of Terra Nova, which he found inside Gidius's chest on the Planet Giddio. Unfortunately Gidius's route is shown on the map using a cunning code.

Guild of Twystian

IGUANA

TERRA

Bokonsrikta

El Taco   Chirpeecheep   Triangula

Turteltitlan

R. Nachos

LLAMALLA

74   76   78   80   82

TERRA

Twystian

0   25 50   100

Friendly Qqvirkans

38

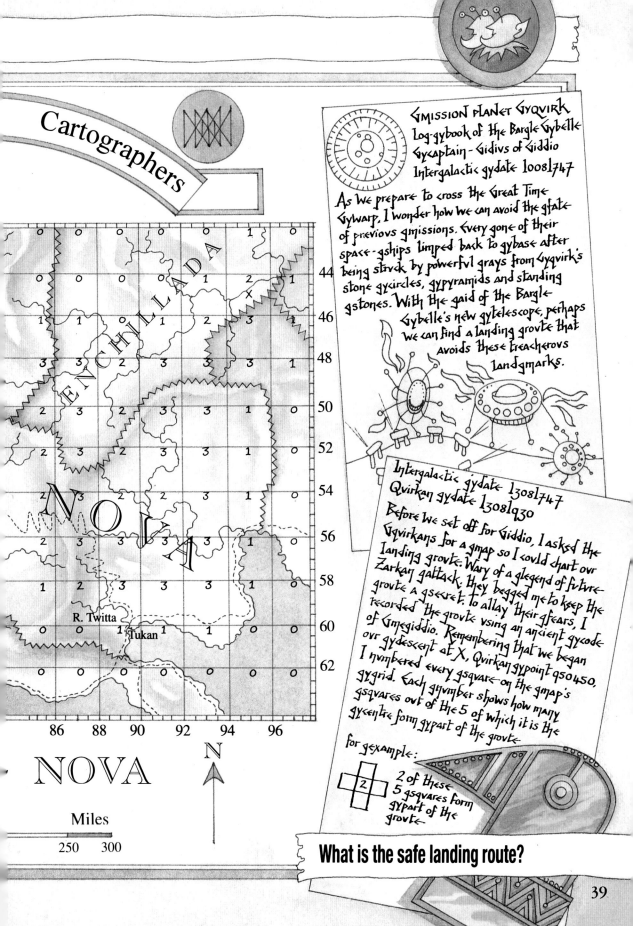

Map grid values (NOVA / ENCHILLADA region)

	86	88	90	92	94	96	
	O	O	O	O	1	O	
	O	O	O	1	2	1	44
	1	1	O	1	3	1	46
	3	3	2	3	3	1	48
	2	3	2	3	3	1	50
	2	3	2	3	3	1	52
	2	3	2	2	3	1	54
	2	3	3	3	3	1	56
	1	2	3	3	3	1	58
	O	O	1	1	1	O	60
	O	O	O	O	O	O	62

R. Twitta
Tukan

ENCHILLADA

NOVA

NOVA

N

Miles

250   300

GMISSION PLANET GYQVIRK
Log-gybook of the Bargle Gybelle
Gycaptain - Gidivs of Giddio
Intergalactic gydate 1008l747

As we prepare to cross the Great Time
Gywarp, I wonder how we can avoid the gfate
of previovs gmissions. Every gone of their
space-gships limped back to gybase after
being strvck by powerful grays from Gyqvirk's
stone gycircles, gypyramids and standing
gstones. With the gaid of the Bargle
Gybelle's new gytelescope, perhaps
we can find a landing grovte that
avoids these treacherovs
landgmarks.

Intergalactic gydate 1308l747
Qvirkan gydate 1308l930

Before we set off for Giddio, I asked the
Gyqvirkans for a gmap so I covld chart ovr
landing grovte. Wary of a glegend of fvtvre
Zarkan gattack, they begged me to keep the
grovte a gsecret. To allay their gfears, I
recorded the grovte vsing an ancient gycode
of Gmegiddio. Remembering that we began
ovr gydescent at X, Qvirkan gypoint q50450,
I nvmbered every gsqvare on the gmap's
gygrid. Each gnvmber shows how many
gsqvares ovt of the 5 of which it is the
gycentre form gypart of the grovte.

for gexample:

2   2 of these
5 gsqvares form
gypart of the
grovte

What is the safe landing route?

The Chart of Loenlinesse

After crossing the Time Warp, Zoonal Duo, Teri Firma and Gygyddion arrived on the Planet Quirk just after the dawn of civilization and brought the Crystal of Leyheyhey to the town of El Taco. Centuries later, an El Tackan sailor, Tikitaka, gave the Crystal to the Hypokondryad who lived in the distant land of Twystia. The Crystal, now known as the Jewel of Joy, was retrieved by Hercula and presented to the people of Harmonika. At the dawn of the Dark Age of the Seven Kingdoms, the Jewel, now called the Singing Rock, was stolen by

A QUESTION OF JEWEL IDENTITY

WHILE bird-watching on the island of Harmonika, Milo Midnight of Middle-Knight-on-Sea stumbled over a chocolate cake plate dating from the dawn of Mythikan civilization.

The platter depicts the mythical heroine Hercula handing the Jewel of Joy to a Harmonikan islander.

According to Prof Ouzo Spurios, the blue Jewel is none other than the Crystal of Leyheyhey, a legendary stone which appears on an ancient Terra Novan carpet, now in Tukan Museum.

CRYSTAL SPACE MISSION

ROSY PARKER, Chief Reporter

EARLY today, Teri Firma of El Taco, Terra Nova, set off across the Time Warp into the Ninth Universe. Her mission is to find the lost Crystal of Leyheyhey.

ALIEN LEGEND

Legend says the Crystal was brought to El Taco by three aliens to protect our planet from destruction by the Planet Zarka.

Teri Firma hopes to travel back in time and beat the alien trio to the Crystal. What will happen next is unclear. In the last 50 years of space exploration, no mission has returned to Quirk.

After crossing the Enchanted Halle of Bombastus's Castle, Syr Gilfryd and Hyldagerd claimed the Singing Rocke and made haste to return to the kingdom of Loenlinesse with their prize. And lo, as they galloped across the Great Bridge of Loenlinesse bearing the magicall Rocke, trees blossomed, flowers bloomed, corn ripened, birdes sang and joy returned at last to that beleaguered lande.

Whenne they reached the Citie of Loenlinesse, Syr Gilfryd and Hyldagerd rode straight to the Great Palace and presented the Singing Rocke to Queen Ethelwalda. The gentle monarch entrusted the Rocke to her loyall counsellor, Vaeralinna the Enchanter, who took it to her tower twixt the Palace and Towne of Midmarsh and locked it in a bejewelled casket.

Sadlie, as the yeares passed, the people of Loenlinesse forgot about the Rocke, the source of their happinesse and prosperitie, and grew idle and selfish. No one repaired Loenlinesse's crumblinge dams and river bankes, or heeded the rising level of the Great Sea. And so one stormie night, Loenlinesse was submerged by a great Flood and her people were forced to seek shelter in neighbouring landes.

ELITE OUTWITTED

LATE last night, Elite Gang leader Lucasta Bombasta was arrested aboard her launch off the Sombrian coast.

Inside Lucasta's luxury launch, detectives found the stolen manuscript, "Ye Great Deeds of Syr Gilfryd" the priceless Mappa Blundi, and a mysterious Dark Age casket.

Other members of the Elite Gang were rounded up in Mascarpone. Police have denied reports that they acted on a tip-off from Terra Nova's Secret Service.

Bombastus of Lollo Rosso. According to "Ye Great Deeds of Syr Gilfryd", the Rock was rescued by Sir Gelfrid and Hildegarde who brought it to the lost land of Loenlinesse. In the Great Gang Era, a descendant of Bombastus, Lucasta Bombasta, recovered an ancient casket from the depths of the Sombrian Sea. It contained this tattered chart of an unknown land, which some believe to be Loenlinesse. Whether the chart holds the secret of the Singing Rock's fate remains a mystery, for no one has been able to decipher its strange writing.

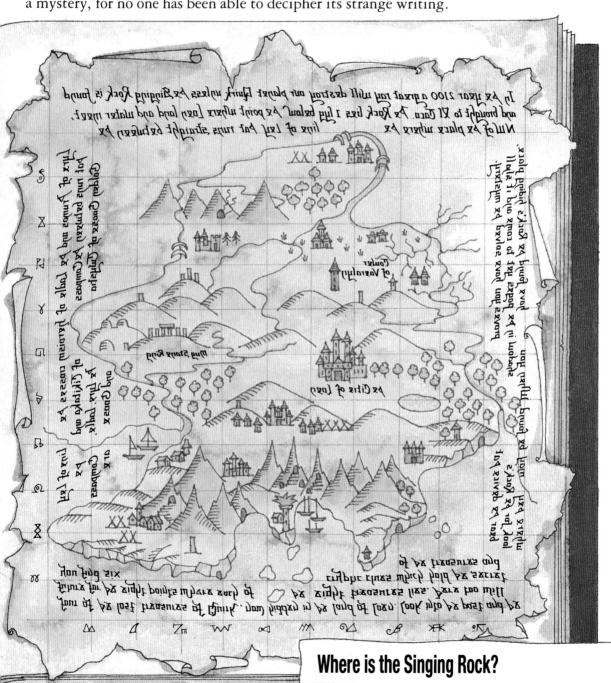

Where is the Singing Rock?

Clues

Page 4
Remember not to follow the same starway twice.

Page 5
Watch out! Some tunnels lead to dead ends.

Page 6
What does the strange inscription on the map plate say? Could Balonius's diary hold the key?

Page 7
Solve this by a process of elimination. Which cities can you rule out? The cryptic clues assume that Mappa Blundi is pointing north.

Page 8
Can you find a route between Via Sinistra and Kriptovia Square that passes through 12 other stations? What time is Mistral's rendezvous?

Page 9
There are only seven moves in the dance, so one dancer can only move once. Remember the dancers may go through several points in one move – even the point they are aiming for.

Page 10
What does the coded message say? Look at the strange design on Orlando Bombasto's locket case. Could it hold the key?

Page 11
Try following Cyclone's directions from each of the towns. Which direction is the map facing?

Pages 12-13
Read the scrolls carefully. Find the secret symbols by a process of elimination then follow them in their correct order. Beware of the curse of Ar.

Pages 14-15
Can you locate the turret cell, the knights' dungeon and the safe hall door on the plan? Where is north? This is a three-dimensional maze.

Pages 16-17
Can you find symbols on the map which match those in the diary?

Pages 18-19
Find the route to the prison on the small map first so you know which major road to aim for on the large map. Look out for the direction arrows at the start of each road.

Pages 20-21
Try combining the words above the pictures of the Casa Fantasa to form a message. Now match up the pictures with the plan. Can you locate most of the rooms using the architect's notes? How many windows does each room have in Mistral's time?

Pages 22-23
Make sure you have a pencil and an eraser.

Pages 24-25
Try each route and make a note of how many geese you gain and lose.

Pages 26-27
Read the diary carefully. Where is the Temple of Pythonia? Can you find a road leading out of the city that is not overlooked by any of the three towers?

Pages 28-29
What are the points of the Megiddion compass? Which direction is the chart pointing?

Pages 30-31
Try putting the tickets in order. Can you find the gangsters' route on the map? Which country are they starting from?

Pages 32-33
Follow the directions from each of the ports of the labyrinth. Where is north?

Pages 34-35
Solve this by a process of elimination. Remember the Path Perilous can only cross a line of squares headed by 1 once. This means that every square forming the path in the previous rows or columns must be found before Gelfrid and Hildegarde can cross these lines.

Pages 36-37
Look at the symbol in the red box at the bottom righthand corner of the map. Could it show which direction the map is pointing? The diagonal lines on the town symbols will help you find the exact locations of El Taco and Chirpeecheep.

Pages 38-39
Once you understand the principle of Gidius's code, the rest is easy.

Pages 40-41
A mirror may be useful. Look back through the book and keep your eyes peeled. Vital information could be lurking anywhere.

Answers

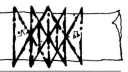

Page 4

Zoonal's route is marked in red.

Page 5

Hercula's route is marked in black.

Page 6

At first glance, the map seems useless, but when Waldo reads Balonius's diary, he realizes that most of the writing is in Turtelese, a language identical to our own but with each word and number written backwards. Translated, the Turtelese inscription on the map plate says:

> The Nachos Region
> Draw two lines from the summits of the four highest mountains. On the point where they cross lies El Taco.
> 12 arms = 1 leg

The four highest mountains are the Heights of Sloth (11 legs), Mount Guacamole (10.1 legs), Jaguar Crest (9.7 legs) and Mount Macaw (9.5 legs). When Waldo draws two lines from their summits, they cross just below Toucan Crest.

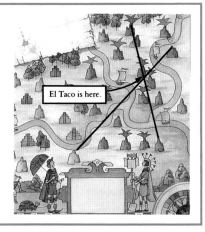

El Taco is here.

Page 7

Sir Gelfrid and Hildegarde locate Lollo Rosso City by a process of elimination. From clue 5, they know that Lollo Rosso City is due south east of Loen City. This means it could be C, D, or G.

If Lollo Rosso City is C, then Loen City must be A. According to clues 1 and 2, Crocodopolis City lies east of Twystia City and south east of Groen City. This means Crocodopolis City can only be D or G. If it is D then Twystia City must be C and Groen City, B. If it is G, then Twystia City can be either E or F and Groen City, A or C. But in each of these cases, Twystia's or Groen's place is occupied by either Lollo Rosso or Loen City, so Lollo Rosso City cannot be C.

If Lollo Rosso City is D, then Loen City must be B. The cities of Crocodopolis, Twystia and Groen can be located at G, at E or F, and at A or C respectively. But this leaves no position free for Mythika City, which lies east of Desperanda City according to clue 3.

This leaves G as the only solution. If Lollo Rosso City is G, then the cities of Crocodopolis, Twystia and Groen are D, C and B respectively. Loen City is A, and Mythika City and Desperanda City are F and E.

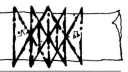

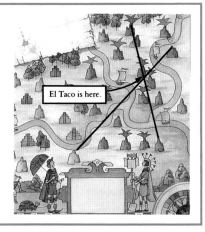

Page 8

Agent Mistral's rendezvous is at Compass Square. This is the ninth of the 12 stations between Via Sinistra and Kriptovia Square and is open at midday.

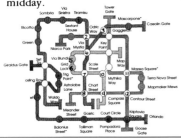

Page 9

These are the seven moves of the Deadly Dance:
1. Hercula moves from A to E
2. Thrumos moves from C to G to A
3. Dogbeast 1 moves from H to D to C to G
4. Dogbeast 2 moves from F to B to H to D to C
5. Hercula moves from E to F to B to H
6. Thrumos moves from A to E to F
7. Dogbeast 1 moves from G to A

Page 10

Waldo decodes the message using the cipher wheel on Orlando Bombasto's locket case. The arrow on the wheel is pointing at A and B. Looking at the message, Waldo realizes that each letter has been substituted by its following letter, so that A becomes B, B becomes C and so on. Decoded, the message says:

The Turquoise Amulet of Twitta is buried under the tree due south of the place where the northernmost of the six statues once stood.

According to the inscription on the plan, none of the six statues stood in vertical, horizontal or diagonal line with any of the others. By a process of elimination, Waldo finds the positions of the four missing statues. These are marked in black. Once he realizes that the plan is pointing west, it is easy to locate the lost amulet.

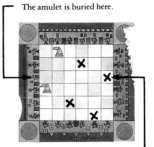

The amulet is buried here.

The northernmost statue.

Page 11

Mistral's route to the message drop is marked in black.

Pages 12-13

Hercula finds the three secret symbols of Ar using a process of elimination. The symbols in their correct order are

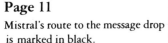

Her route to the Crocodile Crown is marked in black.

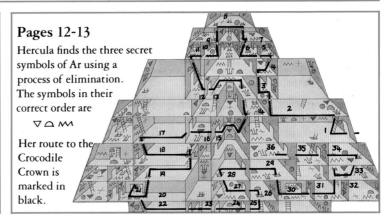

Pages 14-15

Sir Gelfrid and Hildegarde locate their cell and the knights' dungeon by matching the turrets in the picture with those on the plan. The matching turrets are marked with asterisks. The route from the cell to the dungeon is in black, while the route from the dungeon to the safe hall door is in red.

Sir Gelfrid's and Hildegarde's cell.

The knights' dungeon.

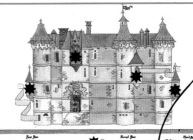

Pages 16-17

According to Balonius, the Triangulans give directions by describing the destination then listing the corners of the triangle in which it is located. The route is a straight line from Triangula. Waldo finds Triangula on the map by looking for a triangle with a symbol inside and symbols at each corner that match those in the diary. Then he finds the city of the Turtels, using the symbols on the diagram to the left of the map. His route between Triangula and the city of the Turtels is marked in red. The symbols are circled in black.

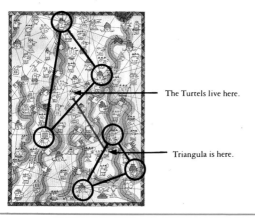

The Turtels live here.

Triangula is here.

Pages 18-19

The route to the Labyrinka Prison is marked in black.

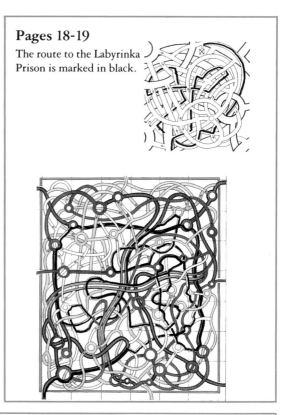

Pages 20-21

First of all, Mistral reads Lucasta's instructions in the correct order. This is what they say:

Walk through three rooms then enter the room with no 'y' in its name and look for the parcel behind the shutter of the third window.

From Cyclone's message, Mistral knows that the layout of the interior of the Casa Fantasa has remained unchanged for 300 years, but the exterior has been altered. She matches up the paintings with the plan, noting how many windows are on each face of the house, according to the pictures, and which direction the plan is pointing. Then Mistral locates most of the rooms on the plan, using the architect's notes. Finally she follows Lucasta's instructions. They lead her through three rooms, the Grand Entrance Hall, the Great Hall and a room which could be the study or the boudoir, into the music room – a room with no 'y' in its name. In Mistral's time, the music room's large single window has been divided into three smaller windows. The parcel is behind the shutter of the third window. Her route is shown in red.

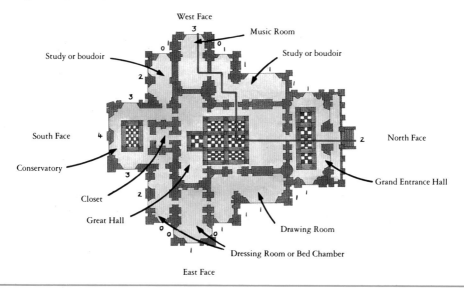

West Face

Music Room

Study or boudoir

Study or boudoir

South Face

North Face

Conservatory

Grand Entrance Hall

Closet

Great Hall

Drawing Room

Dressing Room or Bed Chamber

East Face

Pages 22-23

Hercula's route is shown in black.

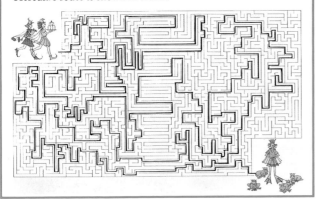

Pages 24-25

Sir Gelfrid's and Hildegarde's route is marked in black. They reach Bombastus's Castle with two surplus geese.

Pages 26-27

From the diary, Waldo learns that Bokonsrikta is deserted during the Pythonic Games except for three guards who have a restricted view of the city from three towers. The streets they can see down are marked in red. Using the description in the diary, Waldo locates the Temple of Pythonia on the plan, then traces the diarist's route to the temple. He remembers that it crossed streets within view of the towers on 11 occasions, when the guards' backs were turned. Once he has escaped from the temple, using the skeleton key, he must retrace this route, marked in black, out of the city.

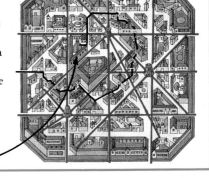

The Temple of Pythonia.

Pages 28-29

Luckily Gidius's directions are easy to translate. In Gmegiddion, all words beginning with a vowel or a consonant, such as F, H, or L, that sounds like a vowel when said out loud, start with "g". All other words start with "gy". The route is marked in black.

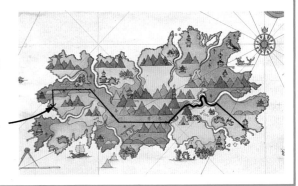

Gidius's chest is buried here.

Pages 30-31

To find the Elite Gang's mystery destination, Mistral puts the airline tickets into their correct order. From Lucasta's letter, she knows that the first airport, Ricotta, is in Mascarpone, the location of the Casa Fantasa (see page 20). Then she finds the Elite Gang's route on the flight chart. This is marked in black and leads to Sombria. Mistral can take a shorter route, shown in red, via Cassata.

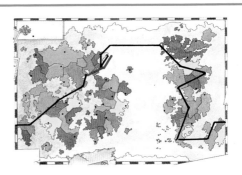

Pages 32-33

Hercula's route is marked in black.

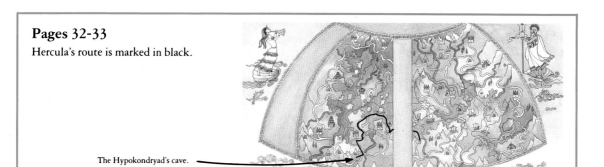

The Hypokondryad's cave.

Pages 34-35

Sir Gelfrid and Hildegarde realize that the Path Perilous can only cross each line of squares headed by a 1 once, so they make sure that they tread on every square of the Path in the previous rows or columns before they cross these lines.

The first part of the Path is easy to find. It goes along the first seven squares in row 7 then up column 7 through two rows headed 1 to row 4.

The Path can't go up to row 2 then down to row 4 as it would need to go up through row 2 for a third time to reach the rows above, so the duo deduce that it must go along four squares in row 4 to column 4.

From there, the Path must pass through the three columns to the left before it can cross column 4 for a third time and go to column 5. First it moves one square to the left into the next column, also a 4, then it goes up just one square to row 6.

From there it can only travel left through column 3 to column 4 and then up through row 3 to row 7. Now all four squares in column 4 have been crossed. Next the Path goes along row 7, completing its passage through columns 3,4 and 4 until it reaches

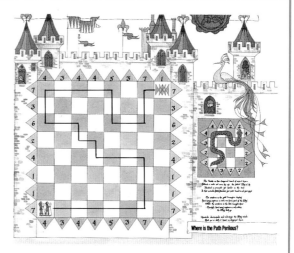

column 5. As only two squares have been crossed in this column, Gelfrid and Hildegarde figure out that the Path must go down through three squares to row 6. To complete row 6, the Path passes through three squares to column 7. Finally, the Path leads up three squares to row 7 and across into column 1 to the Singing Rock.

Pages 36-37

Waldo locates Chirpeecheep and El Taco using the Cheeps' directions and the strange compass. As the symbol in the red box at the bottom of the map matches one of the symbols on the compass, Waldo correctly assumes that it shows the direction the map is pointing. Then he finds the towns using the diagonal lines on each town symbol to calculate his bearings. Now he can plot his route. This is shown in black and the matching pairs of tunnels are numbered in order.

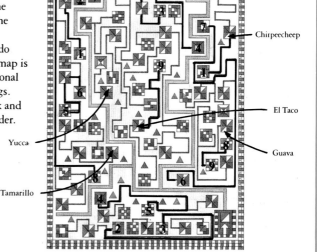

Chirpeecheep

El Taco

Guava

Yucca

Tamarillo

Pages 38-39

Gidius's secret landing route is marked in black.

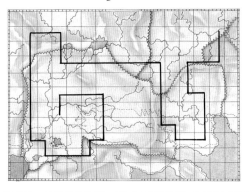

Pages 40-41

Look for the answer elsewhere in this section.

The Strange Story of the Stone

Can you unravel the tangled tale of the stone? All the information lies hidden in the book. Here are some useful hints to point you in the right direction.

6	Where do the people on the map come from?
7	Mappa Blundi could be useful later on.
8	Read the documents carefully. Do some of the names sound familiar? Can you identify a thief? What could the "stone operation" be? Maybe this will make more sense later on.
10	Orlando Bombasto – Lucasta's ancestor?
18-19	Did you read the Declaration? Why is Teri Firma wearing a strange headdress?
20-21	Lucasta seems very interested in the Dark Ages. Do you recognize the symbol above the plan's title?
24-25	Does the name "Bombastus" ring any bells?
26-27	Have you read the letter? Does anything jog your memory? Can you spot a familiar face?
30-31	Did you notice the newspaper clipping? The flight chart is worth studying too. Is there a country missing? What is Lucasta's destination?
32-33	Where does Tikitaka come from? Take a good look at the jewel.
34-35	Have you seen the rock before?
36-37	Did you notice Waldo's new outfit?
38-39	Where will the trio land? Which time zone have they entered?

And Finally . . .

Did you notice:

. . . where Twystia City is on Mappa Blundi? The Twystians believed that their city was in the middle of the Dark Age world. A thousand years earlier, the Mythikan Deities located Harmonika, the heart of early Mythikan civilization, in the middle of their map of the world. Both the Twystians and the Mythikan gods wrongly assumed that the world was flat.

. . . the rivers and some of the places on Balonius's map (page 6), the Triangulan chart (page 17) and the carpet map (page 37) can be matched up with those on the map of Terra Nova (pages 38-39)?

. . . the objects found with the map of Terra Nova? After a long trek through the tunnels of the Nachos Region, Waldo finally reached El Taco where he received a warm welcome and lived happily ever after.

. . . the swagglebird feathers on Lucasta's hat? Orlando Bombasto returned from Terra Nova with a shipload of swagglebirds and made his fortune by selling their bright blue feathers for hats and fans. He then married Marco Niarco's daughter, Sarcasta, and built the Casa Fantasa. As the centuries passed, the poor swagglebirds became rarer and rarer. These gentle fowl, of whom one acted as Vaeralyn's messenger, are now extinct.

. . . the goosey names on Mistral's hiking map? Geese have been held in high esteem in Twystia since the dawn of civilization. The Blue Goose is Twystia's national symbol.

. . . the wavy line on the Twystian metro ticket (page 8) reappears on the Zarkan crest (page 18)? Could the Twystians be the Zarkans' ancestors?

. . . the towers on Mistral's hiking map? These are where the Twystian cartographers lived in accordance with their vows of silence, solitude and secrecy. These eccentric mapmakers left their latest charts in chests outside the towers for lost wayfarers to consult.

. . . the lyre on Balonius's map? When Tikitaka sailed to Harmonika, one of his crew, a Turtel, brought along his lyre. The admiring islanders promptly adopted it as their national instrument.

. . . the stepped pyramid of Ar? This was copied from Tikitaka's drawing of a Terra Novan temple.

. . . if Lucasta found the stone? The Terra Novan Secret Service suspected that this "stone" was none other than the long lost Crystal of Leyheyhey, given to the El Tackans at the dawn of time to protect Quirk from Zarkan attack. They hoped that Lucasta would lead Agent Mistral to the crystal, which would then be returned to El Taco to perform its vital role.

CODES & CIPHERS

Mark Fowler

Designed and illustrated by
Radhi Parekh

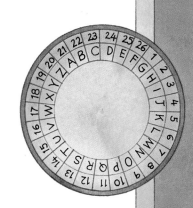

Edited by
Sarah Dixon

Contents

Before You Start

Secret messages, coded diaries, cryptic inscriptions and mysterious symbols . . . all these and more lie in wait on the pages ahead. Some of the puzzles are moderately tricky, while others could prove fiendishly difficult. Look carefully at the documents and illustrations which accompany each puzzle. They contain all the information you require to find the solution. If you need help, turn to pages 90-91 for clues to point you in the right direction. If you are totally stumped, you will find all the answers on pages 92-96.

You can pick out a puzzle to solve at random – if you dare. But if you tackle them in order, you will be able to follow the story of five intrepid adventurers as they grapple with a series of exciting challenges.

WANTED
Five adventurers
Reply with
credentials to
Box No. 15.

The adventure begins when a strange notice appears in the Global Herald. Out of thousands of replies, five individuals are selected to take part in an intriguing mission. They each receive instructions summoning them to Almaro City in the States of Enigma. Clutching packed suitcases and proof of their identity, they report to room 501 of the Rialto Hotel. Here, a mysterious figure in dark glasses checks their credentials . . .

ASSOCIATION OF NEWS JOURNALISTS

OFFICIAL PRESS CARD

NAME: BEN HARVEY
INVESTIGATIVE REPORTER

NEWSPAPER:
THE DAILY PLANET

AXQ-94

PASSPORT
FEDERATION OF THE STATES
OF ENIGMA

Name of bearer: Sally Cameron
Passport no.: 894621 D
Occupation: Explorer

Farmassi
Institute

Name: Carrie Jones PPD,
MKc.
STATUS: Junior research
scientist
DEPARTMENT: Aeronautics

MAODAFI

MACAVITY'S
ACADEMY
OF
DETECTION AND
FORENSIC INVESTIGATION

MEMBERSHIP CARD

NAME: KATE JONSON

TOP SECRET

24-I.I.N.-9

INTERNATIONAL
INTELLIGENCE NETWORK

NAME: MAT SMITH
SECURITY CLEARANCE: ALPHA X2
OPERATIONAL ID: PORTIA 006

The mystery figure hands each person a sealed brown envelope then walks slowly out of the room, leaving a file on a table as he goes. The file contains two small cuttings and a letter . . .

To Mat Smith, Kate Jonson, Ben Harvey, Sally Cameron and Carrie Jones

Let me introduce myself. I am Thomas Hudson, a retired adventurer. After years of painstaking research, I have discovered the location of a hoard of lost treasures from the ancient civilization of the Bilongi Islands. Sadly, my treasure-hunting days are long over, so I am giving you the chance to find the Bilongi treasures.

It will not be an easy task. First, each of you must take on a challenging and possibly dangerous mission:

Mat Smith: you must discover the name of the building where the Red Panther Spy Ring set up its secret headquarters over forty years ago.

Kate Jonson: you must find out where Ben Pierce's gang of Wild West outlaws hid the loot from the Maryville train robbery.

Ben Harvey: you must uncover the true identity of the seventeenth century adventurer known only as Le Capitaine.

Sally Cameron: you must find the name of the mountain where the ancient Bilongi warrior, Hapu, built his stronghold.

Carrie Jones: you must retrieve a coded message from the mountain refuge of the famous mystic, Lo Chi. The message is hidden in Lo Chi's secret chamber.

Each of you has been given a sealed envelope. These contain instructions to lead you to the starting point of your investigations. Do not open your envelope until you have left the hotel and do not reveal its contents to anyone.

You have exactly four weeks to complete your missions. Then you must return to this room at 6pm to take up my ultimate challenge.

Be warned: all five of you must succeed in your tasks. If just one of you fails, you will never discover the secret of the treasures' hiding place.

Good luck,

Thomas Hudson.

WHO'S WHO OF ADVENTURERS
HUDSON, THOMAS: adventurer; born December 9th 1926, Longville; joined International Intelligence Network, 1949; led operation against Red Panther Spy Ring, 1953; set up cattle ranch near San Fernando, 1955; moved to Chateau des Tours, 1960; led expedition to far east, 1974; crash landed on uninhabited island in Bilongi Group, September 1974; located secret refuge of 14th century mystic, Lo Chi, 1975; retired to hermitage in Aldheim Mountains, 1989. PUBLICATIONS: *Le Capitaine: The Man Behind the Myth*. LEISURE INTERESTS: Cryptography; astronomy.

Two thousand years ago, the Bilongi civilization came to an abrupt end when the islands were struck by a series of extremely violent earthquakes. The islanders sailed away in search of new lands. This ancient painting is said to show the Bilongi islanders hiding hundreds of gold and silver treasures before they set sail. These treasures have never been found.

Coded Telegrams

As he hurries away from the Rialto Hotel, secret agent Mat Smith tears open the envelope containing his instructions. Inside, he finds the following message: "LEFT LUGGAGE OFFICE, CENTRAL AIRPORT, ESCOVIA: LOCKER 13". Quickly, Mat hails a taxi and soon he is on his way to the airport. He boards the next plane to the distant republic of Escovia, ready to begin his search for the secret headquarters of the Red Panther Spy Ring.

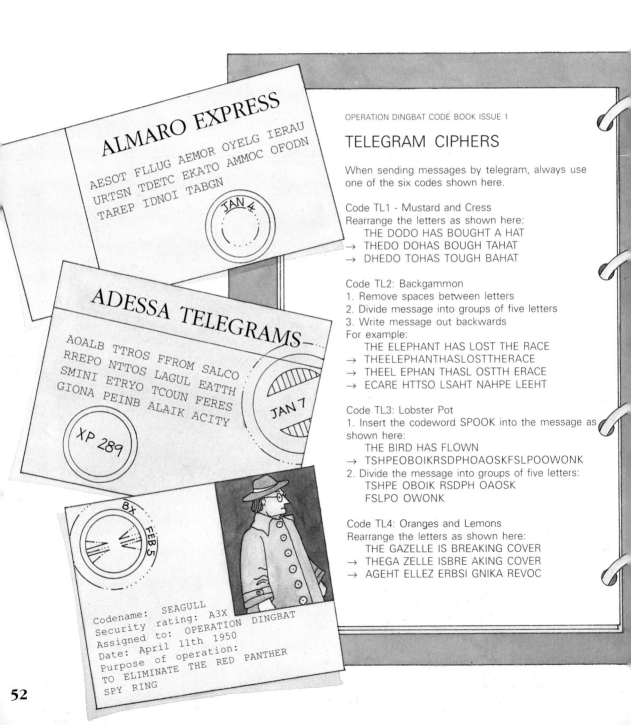

ALMARO EXPRESS

AESOT FLLUG AEMOR OYELG IERAU
URTSN TDETC EKATO AMMOC OFODN
TAREP IDNOI TABGN

JAN 4

ADESSA TELEGRAMS

AOALB TTROS FFROM SALCO
RREPO NTTOS LAGUL EATTH
SMINI ETRYO TCOUN FERES
GIONA PEINB ALAIK ACITY

JAN 7

XP 289

BX
FEB 5

Codename: SEAGULL
Security rating: A3X
Assigned to: OPERATION DINGBAT
Date: April 11th 1950
Purpose of operation:
TO ELIMINATE THE RED PANTHER
SPY RING

OPERATION DINGBAT CODE BOOK ISSUE 1

TELEGRAM CIPHERS

When sending messages by telegram, always use one of the six codes shown here.

Code TL1 - Mustard and Cress
Rearrange the letters as shown here:
    THE DODO HAS BOUGHT A HAT
→ THEDO DOHAS BOUGH TAHAT
→ DHEDO TOHAS TOUGH BAHAT

Code TL2 - Backgammon
1. Remove spaces between letters
2. Divide message into groups of five letters
3. Write message out backwards
For example:
    THE ELEPHANT HAS LOST THE RACE
→ THEELEPHANTHASLOSTTHERACE
→ THEEL EPHAN THASL OSTTH ERACE
→ ECARE HTTSO LSAHT NAHPE LEEHT

Code TL3 - Lobster Pot
1. Insert the codeword SPOOK into the message as shown here:
    THE BIRD HAS FLOWN
→ TSHPEOBOIKRSDPHOAOSKFSLPOOWONK
2. Divide the message into groups of five letters:
    TSHPE OBOIK RSDPH OAOSK
    FSLPO OWONK

Code TL4 - Oranges and Lemons
Rearrange the letters as shown here:
    THE GAZELLE IS BREAKING COVER
→ THEGA ZELLE ISBRE AKING COVER
→ AGEHT ELLEZ ERBSI GNIKA REVOC

Nine hours later, Mat's plane touches down in Escovia.
He makes straight for the left luggage office and retrieves a package from locker 13. It contains a bugging device, an old identity card, a blue file, and five telegrams covered with blocks of meaningless letters. Mat realizes that these are coded messages. Flipping through the file he finds a section headed "Telegram Ciphers". With the help of these pages, he can make sense of the telegrams.

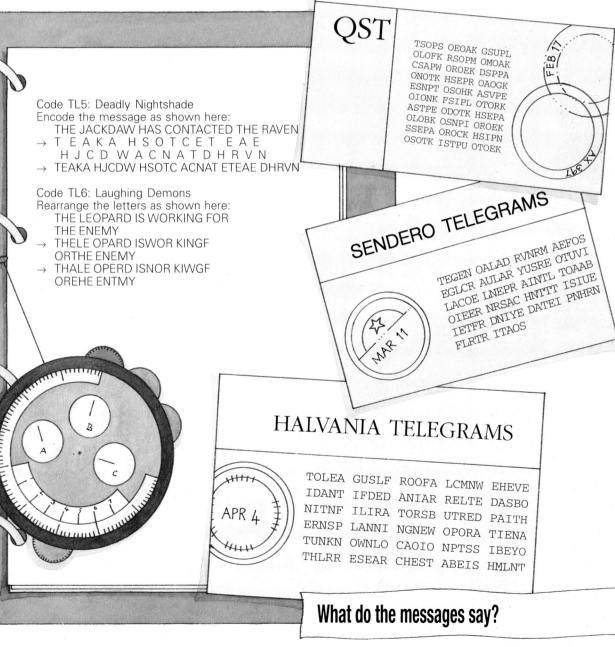

QST

TSOPS OEOAK GSUPL
OLOFK RSOPM OMOAK
CSAPW OROEK DSPPA
ONOTK HSEPR OAOGK
ESNPT OSOHK ASVPE
OIONK FSIPL OTORK
ASTPE ODOTK HSEPA
OLOBK OSNPI OROEK
SSEPA OROCK HSIPN
OSOTK ISTPU OTOEK

FEB 17
AX 397

Code TL5: Deadly Nightshade
Encode the message as shown here:
THE JACKDAW HAS CONTACTED THE RAVEN
→ T E A K A H S O T C E T E A E
   H J C D W A C N A T D H R V N
→ TEAKA HJCDW HSOTC ACNAT ETEAE DHRVN

Code TL6: Laughing Demons
Rearrange the letters as shown here:
THE LEOPARD IS WORKING FOR
THE ENEMY
→ THELE OPARD ISWOR KINGF
  ORTHE ENEMY
→ THALE OPERD ISNOR KIWGF
  OREHE ENTMY

SENDERO TELEGRAMS

TEGEN OALAD RVNRM AEFOS
EGLCR AULAR YUSRE OTUVI
LACOE LNEPR AINTL TOAAB
OIEER NRSAC HNTTT ISIUE
IETFR DNIYE DATEI PNHRN
FLRTR ITAOS

MAR 11

HALVANIA TELEGRAMS

APR 4

TOLEA GUSLF ROOFA LCMNW EHEVE
IDANT IFDED ANIAR RELTE DASBO
NITNF ILIRA TORSB UTRED PAITH
ERNSP LANNI NGNEW OPORA TIENA
TUNKN OWNLO CAOIO NPTSS IBEYO
THLRR ESEAR CHEST ABEIS HMLNT

What do the messages say?

Ben Pierce's Book Cipher

To Danny Heape and Jake Sharp -
We're counting you in on our next
job. In two days time, Joe Gough
will hand you a piece of paper with
your instructions. You must use the
numbers on the piece of paper to
find certain words in the book that I
have enclosed with this letter.
Together, the words form a
message. The numbers will look
something like this:
25.7.6 26.3.8 25.1.5
The first number is a page number.
The second is a line number. The
third is a word number.

Memorize this letter, then
destroy it.

Pierce

GOLD FEVER - CHAPTER 15

BANDITS!

At that moment, Will Gable spotted five horsemen on the hills behind us. "Bandits!" he cried. We leaped back onto the wagon as Will set the horses into a gallop. At once the five horsemen gave chase, racing down the hill toward us.

"Faster!" I cried. "They're gaining on us." We had to reach the safety of the next settlement. We raced along the rough track, sending up a choking column of dust. The noise of the wheels and the horses' hooves was deafening.

Faster and faster we went, the passengers clinging on for dear life as the driver whipped the horses into a frenzy. But the bandits were still gaining on us. The track steepened and to our right it dropped sheer to the valley floor below. The horsemen were now almost upon us. I could see their masked faces and their pistols glinting in the sunlight.

At that moment, we rounded a turn in the track, and there was the small town of Maryville. I heard one of the outlaws cry "Stop!". Then, firing their pistols into the air, they turned and fled.

46

Clutching her envelope, trainee detective Kate Jonson embarks on her search for the place where Ben Pierce and his gang hid the loot from the Maryville train robbery. Kate's instructions contain just five words: "JAKESVILLE: JOE HANK'S GENERAL STORES". After a long train journey, Kate arrives in the small town of Jakesville. At the General Stores, the owner hands her a parcel containing an old book of Wild West memoirs, a letter and a scrap of paper covered with rows of numbers. Reading the letter, Kate quickly realizes that the scrap of paper holds the key to a secret message hidden in the book.

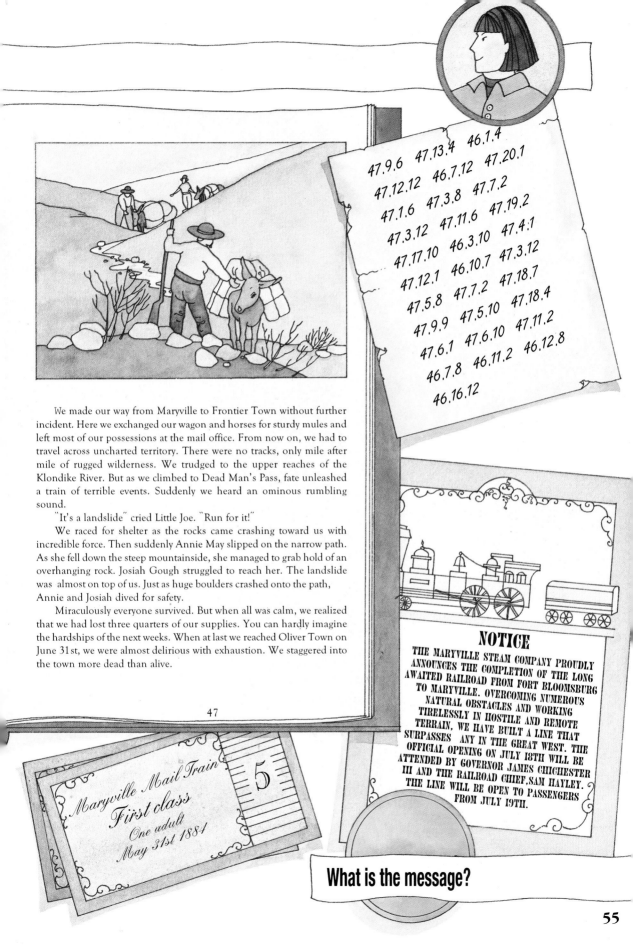

47.9.6 47.13.4 46.1.4
47.12.12 46.7.12 47.20.1
47.1.6 47.3.8 47.7.2
47.3.12 47.11.6 47.19.2
47.17.10 46.3.10 47.4.1
47.12.1 46.10.7 47.3.12
47.5.8 47.7.2 47.18.7
47.9.9 47.5.10 47.18.4
47.6.1 47.6.10 47.11.2
46.7.8 46.11.2 46.12.8
46.16.12

We made our way from Maryville to Frontier Town without further incident. Here we exchanged our wagon and horses for sturdy mules and left most of our possessions at the mail office. From now on, we had to travel across uncharted territory. There were no tracks, only mile after mile of rugged wilderness. We trudged to the upper reaches of the Klondike River. But as we climbed to Dead Man's Pass, fate unleashed a train of terrible events. Suddenly we heard an ominous rumbling sound.

"It's a landslide" cried Little Joe. "Run for it!"

We raced for shelter as the rocks came crashing toward us with incredible force. Then suddenly Annie May slipped on the narrow path. As she fell down the steep mountainside, she managed to grab hold of an overhanging rock. Josiah Gough struggled to reach her. The landslide was almost on top of us. Just as huge boulders crashed onto the path, Annie and Josiah dived for safety.

Miraculously everyone survived. But when all was calm, we realized that we had lost three quarters of our supplies. You can hardly imagine the hardships of the next weeks. When at last we reached Oliver Town on June 31st, we were almost delirious with exhaustion. We staggered into the town more dead than alive.

47

NOTICE

THE MARYVILLE STEAM COMPANY PROUDLY ANNOUNCES THE COMPLETION OF THE LONG AWAITED RAILROAD FROM FORT BLOOMSBURG TO MARYVILLE. OVERCOMING NUMEROUS NATURAL OBSTACLES AND WORKING TIRELESSLY IN HOSTILE AND REMOTE TERRAIN, WE HAVE BUILT A LINE THAT SURPASSES ANY IN THE GREAT WEST. THE OFFICIAL OPENING ON JULY 18TH WILL BE ATTENDED BY GOVERNOR JAMES CHICHESTER III AND THE RAILROAD CHIEF, SAM HAYLEY. THE LINE WILL BE OPEN TO PASSENGERS FROM JULY 19TH.

Maryville Mail Train
First class
One adult
May 31st 1884

5

What is the message?

55

The Playing Card Cipher

To Roland Petanque -
You are summoned to a secret meeting of the Grand
Council of the Montero Society on 5th May to plot
against our newest and most powerful enemy, Le
Capitaine. Use the enclosed items to discover where
the meeting will take place.
1. Look at the top strip of squares on the parchment.
In the third box, you will see the symbols K♥. Take
the King of Hearts. Place it on the message as shown
and note down the circled symbol.

Strip of symbols

Card

2. In the top strip, you will also see the symbols J♣.
Repeat stage 1 using the Jack of Clubs.
3. You now have two symbols. Find these symbols on
the card with the diamond-shaped grid. They form a
reference giving you the first letter of the message.
4. Continue in the same way. Where you see a shorter
strip of squares on the parchment, use the short side of
the relevant playing card.

Henri de la Motte

Ace reporter Ben Harvey sets out to discover the real name of the mysterious
seventeenth century adventurer known only as Le Capitaine. Ben's envelope
contains the following instructions: "OLD MUSEUM, PLACE DE BRIOCHE,
VALERS: CASE 81ZX". At the museum, Ben finds display case 81ZX. Next to a
tattered sheet of parchment and some strange playing cards, he sees an old letter.

The letter reveals that the contents of the case once belonged to a member of a sinister organization called the Montero Society. The members of this society arranged to meet to plot against their sworn enemy, Le Capitaine. Using the parchment and the cards, Ben can discover where the meeting was held.

Where was the meeting?

The Ancient Symbols of Takosu

After nine days on a rusting steamer, intrepid explorer Sally Cameron arrives on Lakala, the only inhabited island in the remote Bilongi Archipelago. She reads through her mission instructions for the hundredth time: "LAKALA ISLAND: THE OLD CUSTOMS HOUSE."

On the waterfront Sally finds the Customs House, long deserted. Inside, she finds a parcel addressed to her. It contains a letter from Thomas Hudson, two pages from a book about ancient Bilongi languages and a parchment covered with strange symbols. From the letter she learns that she must decipher the symbols to begin her search for the place where Hapu built his stronghold over two thousand years ago.

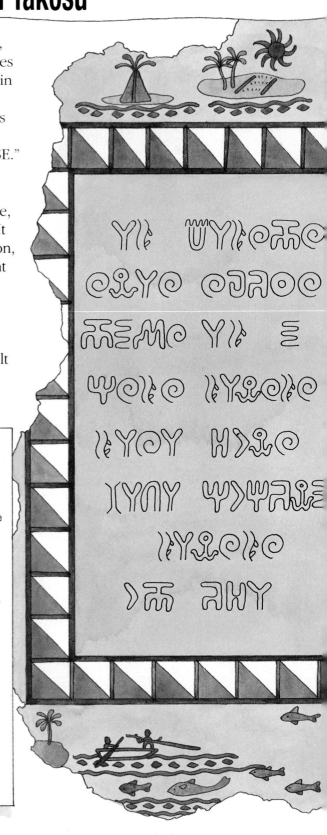

Dear Ms Cameron,

This ancient painting comes from the Bilongi island of Takosu. The symbols in the middle of the painting form a series of sentences in Takosu's ancient language. These reveal the name of the island where Hapu was born. You must translate the symbols then go to the island to continue your quest.

To make sense of the symbols, you must discover which of them corresponds to which English letter. To help you, I enclose two pages from the Official Survey of Ancient Bilongi Languages.

Good luck,

Thomas Hudson.

P.S. When you reach the island where Hapu was born, you must follow the island's only river upstream through thick jungle. After eight miles, you will find a painted stone covered with inscriptions which you must translate.

OFFICIAL SURVEY OF ANCIENT BILONGI LANUAGES. VOLUME 2. The language of Takosu Island. This list includes all the words that were ever written down in this language.

AK	ON
ADUKI	STAR
APOI	DREAMS
BA	SADNESS
BALUNA	KNEW
BENI	WHO
DANUA	FATHER
DO	CHILD
EL	WAS
ENIFI	LONG
GOI	HAPPY
HAPU	HAPU
HI	MOON
IKOLI	SUN
IDOGI	HERO
IGODA	FIRE
IKOALA	MAGIC
INAI	GREAT
JAKILI	MIDSUMMER
KAIA	KAIA
KANIKI	HIS
KATONA	DAY

KOALU	KOALU
KOL	PALM
LAI	DANCE
LO	ABOVE
LUPI	BORN
MATIKI	BROUGHT
MAUI	SILENT
METENA	HEAD
NARANI	BOAT
NOBU	SAW
OA	AND
OANA	OCEAN
OBA	OBA
ONA	FLEW
PALOMA	BRIGHT
PETI	SMALL
RASA	MEANING
RAVALI	KING
RI	ISLAND
SATUMA	FISHERMAN
SO	MOTHER
TAKOI	GREETINGS
TETONU	OF
TIKI	TIKI
U	THE
URAMI	MESSENGER

What do the symbols say?

Lo Chi's Cryptic Board Game

Tearing open her envelope, junior scientist Carrie Jones finds the following message: "LAPSANG TEA WAREHOUSE, SAITONG: ASK FOR HOO MING". After a long journey, Carrie arrives in the far eastern city of Saitong, the starting point of her search for Lo Chi's secret refuge. She hurries through a maze of backstreets to the Lapsang warehouse and steps inside a vast, deserted storeroom. "Hoo Ming?" she calls nervously.

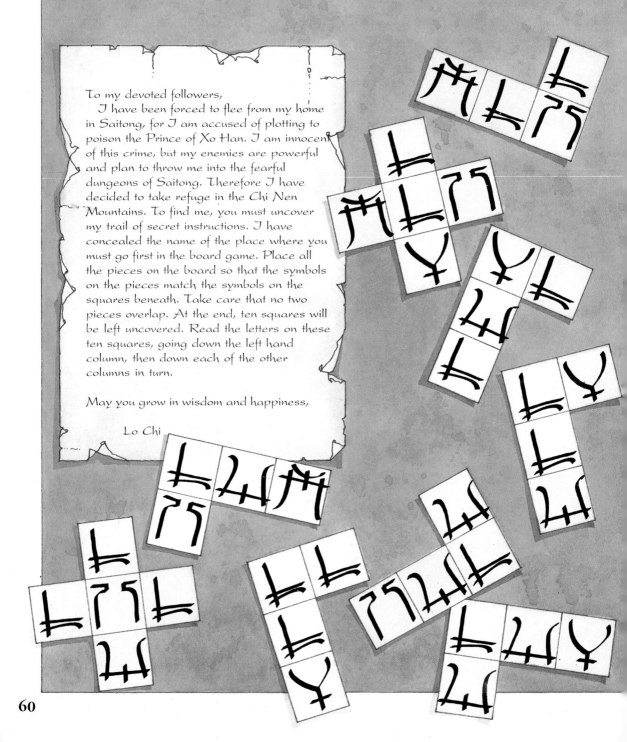

To my devoted followers,
   I have been forced to flee from my home in Saitong, for I am accused of plotting to poison the Prince of Xo Han. I am innocent of this crime, but my enemies are powerful and plan to throw me into the fearful dungeons of Saitong. Therefore I have decided to take refuge in the Chi Nen Mountains. To find me, you must uncover my trail of secret instructions. I have concealed the name of the place where you must go first in the board game. Place all the pieces on the board so that the symbols on the pieces match the symbols on the squares beneath. Take care that no two pieces overlap. At the end, ten squares will be left uncovered. Read the letters on these ten squares, going down the left hand column, then down each of the other columns in turn.

May you grow in wisdom and happiness,

   Lo Chi

An old man emerges from the shadows and hands Carrie a wooden box. She opens the box and carefully lifts out an old game board, thirteen game pieces and a yellowed letter. The letter reveals that four hundred years ago, Lo Chi left a trail of cryptic instructions so that his followers could find their way to his secret refuge. The first set of instructions are concealed in the boardgame.

What do the instructions say?

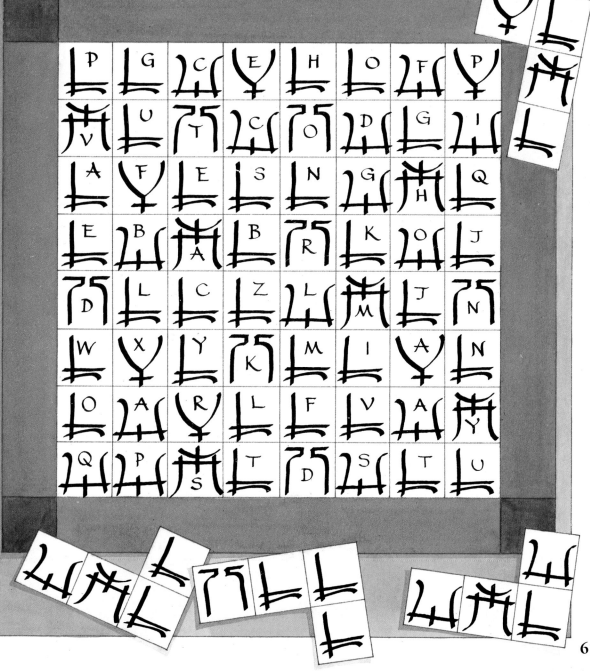

Scrambled Symbols

Acting on information in the coded telegrams, Mat Smith goes to the Ministry of Counter Espionage in the North Escovian city of Balaika. Forty years ago, this was the base for a secret operation codenamed Dingbat which aimed to smash the Red Panther Spy Ring. Ministry officials check Mat's identity, then lead him to the Archive Rooms, deep underground. Mat searches among shelves of dusty files and finally unearths a battered folder marked DINGBAT PHASE 2.

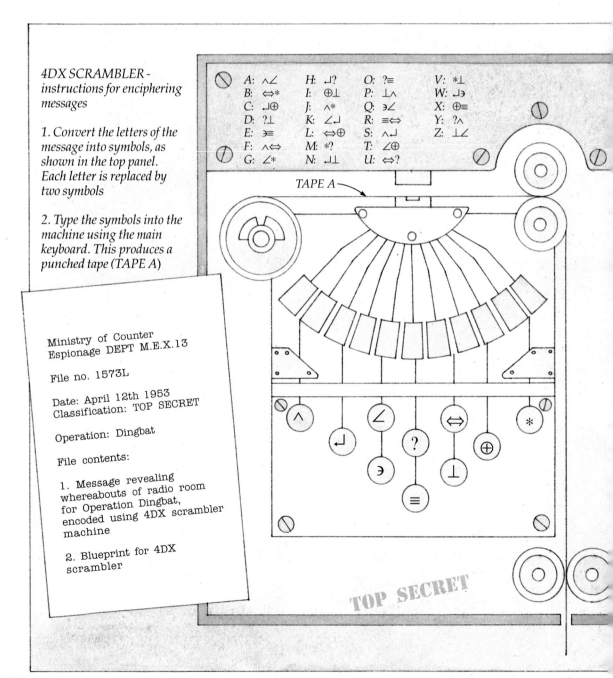

4DX SCRAMBLER - instructions for enciphering messages

1. Convert the letters of the message into symbols, as shown in the top panel. Each letter is replaced by two symbols

2. Type the symbols into the machine using the main keyboard. This produces a punched tape (TAPE A)

A: ∧∠	H: ⌐?	O: ?≡	V: *⊥
B: ⇔*	I: ⊕⊥	P: ⊥∧	W: ⌐ⱻ
C: ⌐⊕	J: ∧*	Q: ⱻ∠	X: ⊕≡
D: ?⊥	K: ∠⌐	R: ≡⇔	Y: ?∧
E: ⱻ≡	L: ⇔⊕	S: ∧⌐	Z: ⊥∠
F: ∧⇔	M: *?	T: ∠⊕	
G: ∠*	N: ⌐⊥	U: ⇔?	

TAPE A

Ministry of Counter Espionage DEPT M.E.X.13

File no. 1573L

Date: April 12th 1953
Classification: TOP SECRET

Operation: Dingbat

File contents:

1. Message revealing whereabouts of radio room for Operation Dingbat, encoded using 4DX scrambler machine

2. Blueprint for 4DX scrambler

TOP SECRET

Inside, he finds two strips of paper punched with symbols and a blueprint for an ingenious scrambler machine. The strips of paper were produced by the scrambler and reveal the location of a secret radio room used for Operation Dingbat. If Mat works through the encoding instructions on the blueprint in reverse order, he can make sense of the symbols.

What do the symbols say?

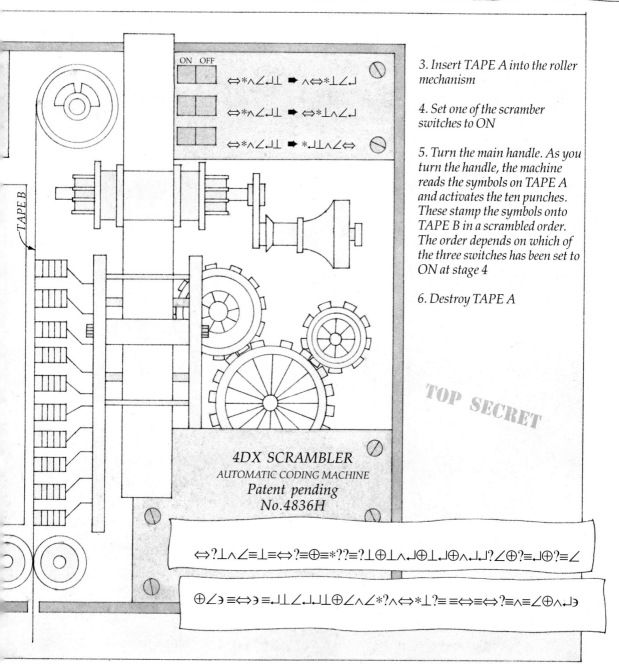

3. Insert TAPE A into the roller mechanism

4. Set one of the scramber switches to ON

5. Turn the main handle. As you turn the handle, the machine reads the symbols on TAPE A and activates the ten punches. These stamp the symbols onto TAPE B in a scrambled order. The order depends on which of the three switches has been set to ON at stage 4

6. Destroy TAPE A

TOP SECRET

4DX SCRAMBLER
AUTOMATIC CODING MACHINE
Patent pending
No.4836H

Joe Gough's Coded Diary

From Ben Pierce's coded message, Kate Jonson knows that the attack on the Maryville mail train was led by an outlaw called Joe Gough. At the library in Jakesville, Kate hunts through a collection of old copies of the Western Star newspaper in search of more information. From these, she learns that Gough was arrested in 1885. In his possession was a coded diary which is now kept at the James Chichester Museum in the bustling city of San Fernando.

Kate sets out on the long journey to San Fernando. At the museum, she finds the diary in a display case. It is open at the entry for May 31st 1884, the day of the attack on the train. With the help of a label in the case and a strange coding device, Kate can decipher the entry.

JOE GOUGH – LEGENDARY OUTLAW

Joe Gough was a member of Ben Pierce's band of outlaws, who terrorized the Maryville territories from 1865 until 1885. The gang became notorious when they held up the Maryville mail train in 1884, stealing a large consignment of gold bound for the San Fernando Bank. The gold was finally recovered thirty years ago by local rancher, Tom Hudson.

It is thought that Gough was the brains behind the gang's activities. He started in life as a lawyer, but when he was accused of corruption in 1872, he fled into the Red Mountains where he joined Pierce's gang. His diary provides a fascinating account of the outlaw's life. It is written in an elaborate code. First Gough changed the punctuation then he scrambled the order of the lines in the entry with the help of an unusual coding device.

May '31st 84

♣ *Distant engine*
signal! We'd attack
would force the driver. To stop at their
minutes … Later the train came into view
the mail van. And grabbed the sacks
I set off. With Hank Knott at sunrise and
Heape and Jake Sharp! Were aboard and
Davenport. We raced back to our horses
of gold.
"Prepare," to strike. I yelled at Hank:
"Pass waiting for the train!" to appear at
we took up. Our positions in the Klondike.
Halt the plan was working. We rushed -
we both knew. The plan by heart Danny
were led. By our old enemy marshal. Jack
(the train) screeched to a sudden
noon exactly. We heard the sound of a
horsemen riding in our direction. They
but at that moment I saw a column of -
"To the train!" smashed open the doors of
♦ *Davenport. Rode straight at him. Hank*
tore along the mountain trails, driving.
But Davenport was hot on our heels. We

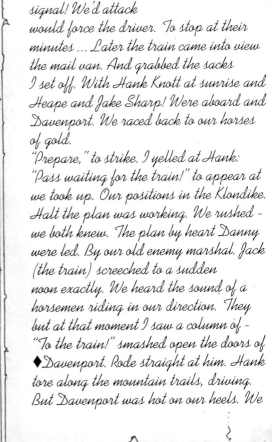

WANTED
DEAD OR ALIVE

was in the marshal's clutches ...
For the secret hideaway, but when we
loot in a secret. Place then fled into the
horses. And galloped away from the scene
location of our hideaway. We buried the
arrived Pierce. Was waiting for us with
scrambled to his feet, but seconds later he
(staggering under the weight of the gold)
next county.
Last we managed to outride. Our pursuers
the rest of us leaped back. Onto our
he had even. Handed over details of the
our horses as hard as we could. And at
suddenly I saw Hank Knott stumble
to Fort Davenport. And had betrayed us
bad news. Hank Knott had been. Taken
we laid low until nightfall then set out.

...OUGH

...OUS OUTLAW

Elaborate coding device used by Joe Gough to encipher his diary

Original line number																			
1	2	3	4	5	6	7	8	9	10	11	12	13	14	15	16	17	18	19	20
19	18	15	8	6	12	11	17	1	10	4	14	7	3	2	16	13	20	5	9	19 18 15 8 6 12

Coded line number

♠ ♥ ♣ ♦
♠ ♥ ♣ ♦

What does the diary say?

The Montero Meeting

To Henri Mayenne,

You are hereby appointed as official secretary to the worthy Society of Montero. You will keep a record of all Montero Society activities. Meetings of the Grand Council shall be recorded in code using the following method:
-- remove all spaces and punctuation from the matter to be encoded
- replace the letters A, E, I, O and U with numbers or symbols. Select three different numbers or symbols to stand for each letter. Each time you encode a letter, use any one of the three relevant numbers or symbols.

By the order of the Duke of Thierry, Grand Master of the Montero Society

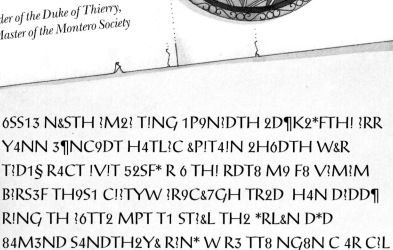

6SS13 N&STH !M2! T!NG 1P9N!DTH 2D¶K2*FTH! !RR
Y4NN 3¶NC9DT H4TL!C &P!T4!N 2H6DTH W&R
T!D1§ R4CT !V!T 52SF* R 6 TH! RDT8 M9 F8 V!M!M
B!RS3F TH9S1 C!!TYW !R9C&7GH TR2D H4N D!DD¶
R!NG TH !6TT2 MPT T1 ST!&L TH2 *RL&N D*D
84M3ND S4NDTH2Y& R!N* W R3 TT8 NG8N C 4R C!L
L2 P R!S 1N T H9 D §K! D!M6 ND!D TH6T W!

From the playing card message, Ben Harvey knows that the members of the sinister Montero Society met at Chateau Lot over four hundred years ago to plot against their arch enemy, Le Capitaine. Ben travels to the chateau, hoping to find out more. When he arrives, he explains his mission to the present owner, the Countess of Montmorency.

D5SC*V!R TH! !D !NT!TY*F L! C4P!T& !N!S1T H4TW!
C6N! L8M5 N&T! H5M 1NC!4NDF* RALL.5MM !D!&T
!LYR *L4N D P!T6N Q7! L! &P!D T 1 H!S F !2T 4NN
*§NC!N G TH &T H9H&D H!R9D 6 C!RT4!N M
*NS8!7R TH3M 6 ST*D8S C*V!R H!S TR¶! !D2N T!TY
M*NS!!¶RTH3M6S !S *N! 1FT H!M1ST C ¶N N!NG
R3G§!S !NTH!W H*L! K8 NGD1 M TH! D¶K2 W6
SPL! 4S!D &T T H9 N!WS& ND 3FF!R !D T* R!W 6RD M
*NS52§RT H3M 6SW!THF5 V2 H§NDR! DFR6N CS5FH!
S¶C C !9DS

Monsieur Thomas
Fencing Master
31, Rue de la Pique

In the large library, the countess hands Ben a leather bound book, which falls open at a page covered with strange writing. The countess explains that the page contains coded details of the secret meeting. With the help of a letter that he finds tucked inside the cover, Ben can decipher the writing.

What does the writing say?

The Mystery of the Tiki Inscriptions

Sally Cameron has discovered that the warrior Hapu was born on the island of Tiki. Now she must set sail for this island and follow its only river upstream to find a painted stone.

Armed with charts and helpful notes from the Bilongi Institute of Exploration, Sally reaches Tiki and slowly rows up the river. She abandons her boat at the foot of a waterfall and hacks her way through the thick jungle that lies along the bank. Scratched, bruised and close to exhaustion, she finally reaches the stone. On it is painted a snake decorated with strange inscriptions. With the help of her notes, Sally can translate the inscriptions into English.

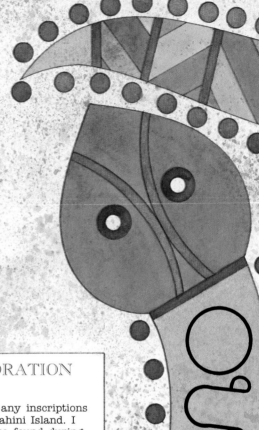

What do the inscriptions say?

THE BILONGI INSTITUTE OF EXPLORATION

Dear Sally,
We have no record of inscribed stones on Tiki Island, but any inscriptions would be in the same language that was used on nearby Tahini Island. I enclose a copy of some Tahini Island inscriptions that were found during a recent expedition. Each symbol corresponds to one English word, but the order of words is not the same as in English.
I hope this information will help you in your mission,

Anita Kaia

Head of Exploration.

Tahini Island Inscriptions	Translation
	Kinja gave a papaya to Hapu
	The earthquake destroyed the temple
	The evil magician left the islanders
	Oba sang to Kaia
	Adiki struck Oba
	Adiki sailed away
	A firebird came to Tiki
	One firebird gave a seashell to Kinja
	Another firebird went to Guana
	Oba went to the temple
	Kaia ruled the islanders
	One group sang to Hapu
	The fearsome magician led the dance
	Kinja left Guana

The Grids of Go

To my devoted followers,

To find my next set of instructions, you must use the papers that you will find with this letter. They consist of four square grilles, a grid of letters stamped with the seal of my friend the Prince of Go, and a large scroll of symbols.

- Look at the first symbol on the scroll. (You will find the first symbol in the top left hand corner)
- Find the grille with this symbol in the corners
- Lay the grille over the grid of letters
- Take the letter that lies beneath the number 1 on the grille. This is the first letter of the message
- Do the same for the second symbol on the scroll (the second symbol is underneath the first)
- Use the same method to reveal the rest of my message. When you come to a symbol for the second time, lay the grille over the grid of letters as before, but take the letter under the number 2
- When you reach the end of the first column on the scroll, translate the symbols in the second column.

May you grow in wisdom and prosperity,

Lo Chi

O	G	H	T	P	G	O
O	T	E	A	O	D	O
A	M	H	E	I	A	X
F	N	N	I	F	T	N
N	D	D	H	K	E	R
E	E	E	T	F	O	R
P	E	O	B	H	S	E

The message hidden in Lo Chi's cryptic board game directs Carrie Jones to the Grand Palace in the ancient city of Go. After an almost endless journey across the plains of Lo Sung, she arrives at Go's Main Station. She makes straight for the Grand Palace where she finds a collection of objects and papers that once belonged to Lo Chi.

They consist of a scroll with elaborate symbols, a letter, four cards with number grids and a page with a grid of letters. Following instructions in the letter, Carrie can discover where Lo Chi hid the next set of instructions in the trail leading to his secret refuge.

Where are the instructions hidden?

Morse Transmission

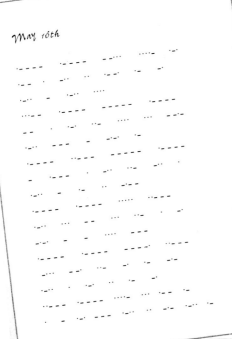

May 16th

Mat Smith makes his way through the Kamarov Forest to the ruined tower used by Dingbat agents over forty years ago. Inside the tower, he finds a trapdoor. It opens to reveal a flight of steps leading down to a small underground chamber. On an old desk, Mat spots a piece of paper covered with dots and dashes, together with a code book, an old newspaper and a radio transmitter. The dots and dashes form a secret message. With the help of the code book and the newspaper, Mat can figure out exactly what it says.

What does the message say?

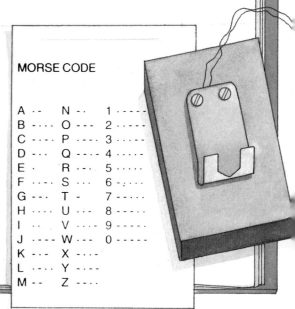

OPERATION DINGBAT
CODE BOOK ISSUE 2

CODE 4976: HAIRPIN BENDS

ENCODING INSTRUCTIONS

1. Remove all punctuation and word spaces from the message.
2. Divide the text into GROUPS of eight letters.
3. Select a four letter KEYWORD from the previous day's Global Herald. It must not contain any letters that appear in the first eight letter GROUP of the message.
4. Write down a REFERENCE for the KEYWORD. A typical REFERENCE looks like this: 2 23 4. This means that the KEYWORD is in the second column, line 23 and is the 4th word in the line. When counting the line numbers, do not include the newspaper's title, headlines, headings, or subheadings.
5. Take the first KEYWORD and the first GROUP of letters and scramble them. For instance, if the first GROUP was MEETINGS and the first KEYWORD was LOCK, the jumbled version could be MLEEOTICNGSK.
6. Write down the scrambled KEYWORD and eight letter GROUP after the REFERENCE.

7. Select a second KEYWORD, making sure that it does not include any letters that appear in the second eight letter GROUP of the message, and write down its REFERENCE. Scramble the KEYWORD with the second GROUP of letters, then write them down after the reference.
8. Continue in the same way until the whole message is encoded. Then translate everything into Morse Code, and transmit on frequency GF7.

MORSE CODE

A ·—	N —·	1 ·————
B —···	O ———	2 ··———
C —·—·	P ·——·	3 ···——
D —··	Q ——·—	4 ····—
E ·	R ·—·	5 ·····
F ··—·	S ···	6 —····
G ——·	T —	7 ——···
H ····	U ··—	8 ———··
I ··	V ···—	9 ————·
J ·———	W ·——	0 —————
K —·—	X —··—	
L ·—··	Y —·——	
M ——	Z ——··	

15th May 1953

Issue no. 1756

THE GLOBAL HERALD

RED PANTHER STRIKES BALAIKA CITY

A RELIABLE SOURCE LAST NIGHT DISCLOSED THAT A SINISTER SPY RING IS OPERATING IN BALAIKA CITY. Members of an organization calling itself the Red Panther Ring have infiltrated the world famous Pyrites Research Institute. They have stolen top secret formulas which could enable them to hold the entire country to ransom. The spies are said to be extremely well organized and highly dangerous.

Reports suggest that the spy ring may be led by the notorious criminal mastermind, Lev Sapova. Wanted on numerous counts of conspiracy and espionage, Sapova is undoubtedly the most dangerous – and elusive – criminal operating in Escovia today.

UNDERCOVER INVESTIGATION

It is understood that an undercover investigation is being carried out by agents from the International Intelligence Network. However, as each day passes, the dangers increase. The leaders of the Red Panther must be caught before they strike again.

CONTENTS

REGATTA RETURNS

The much loved soprano Carlotta Regatta has announced that she will come out of retirement for a gala performance on July 8th at the Borlotti Opera House.

MYSTERY HEIR SOUGHT

Lawyers are still trying to trace a descendant of the seventeenth century adventurer, Le Capitaine. The mystery descendent has inherited the magnificent Chateau des Tours in the world famous Amouret Valley. He is thought to live somewhere in the States of Enigma, but so far all attempts to trace him have failed.

NEWS IN BRIEF

World famous detective, Archie Malloy has been awarded the Order of Merit for solving the case of the Sarga

Explorers in Bis
that they h
Mammot ous
that the ike anim
had bee usands of years

Cut Out Letters

Jackson's Cave

Stoker's Cavern

Kutter's Canyon

Stetson Cave

Lone Creek Cavern

THe MoON sHInEs briGHTly ovEr muStaNg prAIrie

To Hank Knott.
Meet me at my hideaway after the attack on the train. Use the disks that Joe Gough gave you to find the hidden words in the enclosed message. They reveal the location of the hideaway.
- Each letter of the alphabet is given a 3-digit number as shown on the large disk. Some numbers have worn off, so you will have to fill these in for yourself.
- Each digit corresponds to a different letter height in the coded message, as shown on the small disk.
Memorize the contents of this letter then destroy it.
Pierce

Hank Knott

Faraway Farm

Demon's Creek

Lone Cave

In San Fernando, Kate Jonson discovers that a member of Pierce's gang was captured by Marshal Davenport during the attack on the Maryville mail train. He was taken to Davenport's headquarters at Fort Chichester where he betrayed his fellow bandits. Kate travels to the fort, now carefully restored, where some belongings of the captured outlaw are on display. Among them are a letter, two metal disks and a scrap of paper with a sentence made up from cut out printed letters. Behind the innocent words, there is a cunningly concealed message.

What is the hidden message?

The Fencing Master's Papers

Ben Harvey knows that a character called Monsieur Thomas was hired by the Montero Society to discover the real identity of their arch enemy, Le Capitaine. Monsieur Thomas ended his days as fencing master to the Regiment of Muskateers. At the regiment's modern headquarters, Ben unearths objects and papers that once belonged to Monsieur Thomas. They include two game counters, a letter and a picture covered with symbols.

What do the symbols say?

To Monsieur Thomas
You must leave all communications to the Montero Society at a secret message point. The enclosed engraving contains a coded message revealing the location of this place. To decode it you will need the two patterned counters that we gave you at the start of your mission. The message consists of five bands of symbols, each divided into two rows. First translate the symbols into letters. Use the counter with the symbol ⊗ to translate the symbols in the top row, and the counter with the symbol ☆ for the bottom row. Once all the symbols are translated, read along each band to uncover the message.
R.P.

The Jumbled Symbols of Guana

OFFICIAL SURVEY OF ANCIENT BILONGI LANGUAGES –
VOLUME 6, APPENDIX 4

GUANA ISLAND - ANCIENT SYMBOLS

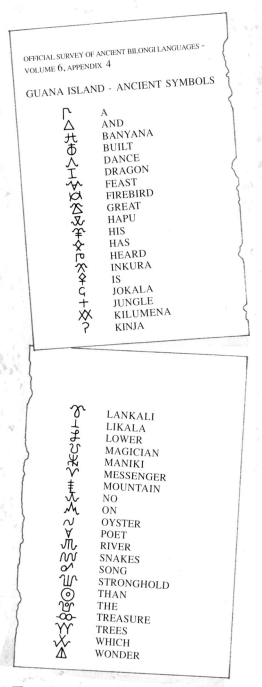

A
AND
BANYANA
BUILT
DANCE
DRAGON
FEAST
FIREBIRD
GREAT
HAPU
HIS
HAS
HEARD
INKURA
IS
JOKALA
JUNGLE
KILUMENA
KINJA

LANKALI
LIKALA
LOWER
MAGICIAN
MANIKI
MESSENGER
MOUNTAIN
NO
ON
OYSTER
POET
RIVER
SNAKES
SONG
STRONGHOLD
THAN
THE
TREASURE
TREES
WHICH
WONDER

From the inscriptions on the snake painting, Sally Cameron knows that Hapu left the island of Tiki and set course for distant Guana Island. Is this where he set up his legendary stronghold? Sally returns to her boat and sails to Guana. Exploring the island's shores, she comes across a stone marked with an arrow. Further along the beach, she finds another, and soon she is following a winding trail.

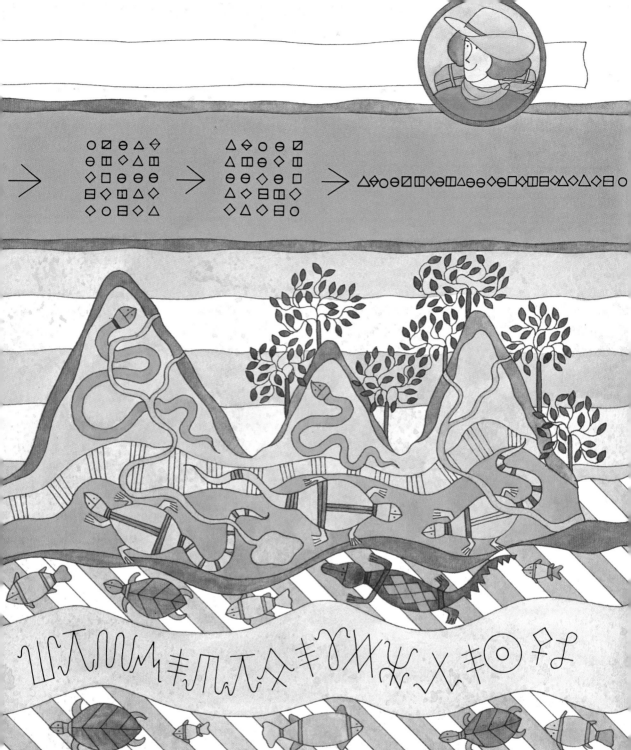

The trail ends at a cave where Sally finds an ancient painting of the island. A row of pictograms runs below the painting. With the help of her notes, Sally translates the symbols into English, but the words are strangely jumbled. Could the patterns above the painting reveal how they have been rearranged?

What do the symbols say?

The Secret of the Chart

Following in the footsteps of Lo Chi, Carrie Jones sets out for the pagoda of Ho Min Xen, high on the plateau of Noh. When she reaches the pagoda, she finds that it is now in ruins, and there is no sign of Lo Chi's message. Carrie goes to the nearby village of Chang Xi, where she discovers that a hundred years ago a band of marauders looted the pagoda. Many of the stolen treasures were lost forever, but a few were recovered and are now kept at the village.

To my devoted followers,

You are nearing the end of your journey. The dial and papers that you will find with this letter conceal the name of the remote mountain village where I have left my final set of instructions.
- Look at the first column of symbols on the piece of paper below. The top symbol is a full circle, and underneath is the symbol ⊟. Find the full circle on the chart, then the symbol ⊟ around its rim. Draw an imaginary line from the middle of the circle, through the symbol ⊟ and across the chart.
- Return to the paper below. Repeat the process for the two symbols at the bottom of the first column.
- You now have two imaginary lines crossing the chart. Where the two lines meet you will find a symbol.
- Set the dial so that ⊟ = H, and find the letter that corresponds to the symbol you have found on the chart.
- Continue until the message is revealed.

May you grow in wisdom and happiness,
Lo Chi

Sorting through the recovered treasures, Carrie finds a collection of papers and objects hidden in the folds of a silk painting. Excitedly, she spots a letter signed by Lo Chi, together with a dial, a small scroll and a complex chart. The letter tells her that these curious objects conceal a secret message revealing the name of the village where Lo Chi left his final instructions.

What is the name of the village?

The Dingbat File

From the message in the secret radio room, Mat Smith knows that Dingbat agents sent details of the location of the Red Panther headquarters to a special bunker in the city of Satroika. Mat takes the midnight plane to Satroika. With the help of contacts in the secret service, he discovers that the bunker is still in use. He finds his way there and explains his mission to the Head of Operations who leads him through a maze of corridors to the Central Control Room.

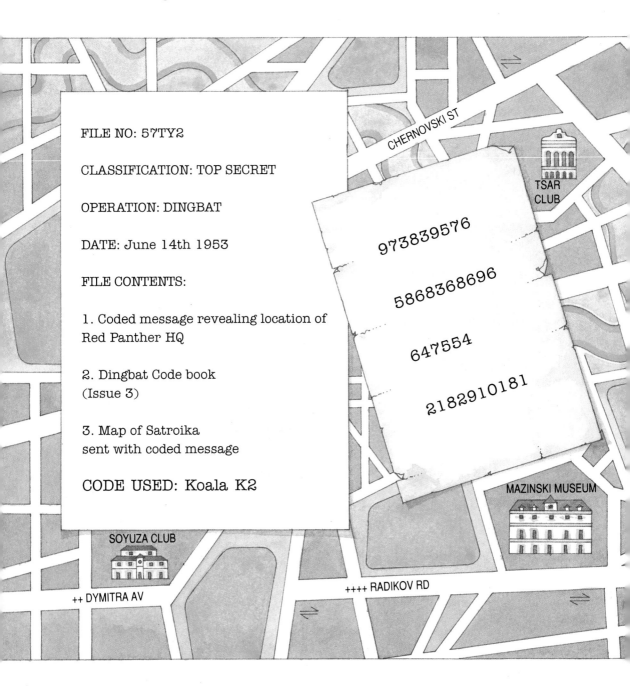

FILE NO: 57TY2

CLASSIFICATION: TOP SECRET

OPERATION: DINGBAT

DATE: June 14th 1953

FILE CONTENTS:

1. Coded message revealing location of Red Panther HQ

2. Dingbat Code book (Issue 3)

3. Map of Satroika sent with coded message

CODE USED: Koala K2

973839576

5868368696

647554

2182910181

CHERNOVSKI ST

TSAR CLUB

MAZINSKI MUSEUM

SOYUZA CLUB

++ DYMITRA AV

++++ RADIKOV RD

Here, he is handed a file marked DINGBAT:TOP SECRET. The file contains a typed card, a code book, a street map and a piece of paper with rows of numbers on it. The numbers form a coded message. With the help of instructions in the code book, Mat can decipher the message and at last locate the secret headquarters of the Red Panther Ring.

Where are the headquarters?

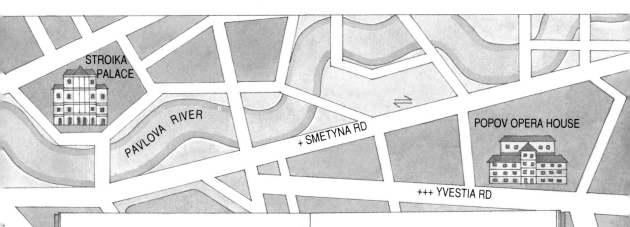

STROIKA PALACE

PAVLOVA RIVER

+ SMETYNA RD

POPOV OPERA HOUSE

+++ YVESTIA RD

OPERATION DINGBAT:
CODE BOOK ISSUE 3

Code 15: KOALA K2

Brief description:
Koala K2 is a grid based code
involving keywords.

Encoding instructions:
1. The basic grid for Koala K2
looks like this:

```
   1 2 3 4 5 6 7
 8 □ □ □ □ □ □ □
 9 □ □ □ □ □ □ □
 0 □ □ □ □ □ □ □
   □ □ □ □ □
```

Choose a series of keywords.
Each keyword must contain seven
different letters, and can be
taken from any document.
Enclose the document with the
coded message and mark the
first keyword with the symbol
+, the second with the symbols
++, the third with the symbol
+++ and so on.

Write the first keyword along
the top row of the grid. Then
write out the remaining letters
of the alphabet in the spaces
below. This is how the grid
would look if the keyword was
LEOPARD:

```
   1 2 3 4 5 6 7
   L E O P A R D
 8 B C F G H I J
 9 K M N Q S T U
 0 V W X Y Z
```

2. Translate the letters of the
message into numbers. Letters
in the top row of the grid are
replaced by the number above
them. In the LEOPARD grid, L=1,
E=2 etc. Letters in the other
rows are replaced by two
numbers: the number at the
beginning of the row, followed
by the number at the top of the
column. In the LEOPARD grid
B=81, C=82 etc.

3. Change the keyword every
six letters. You will need
to draw a new grid for each
new keyword.

Sam Hayley's Cipher

May 30th – Sam Hayley's message arrived this morning. As arranged, he wrote it in code. Using his grid, I have deciphered the information and now I am ready to plan the attack.

May 31st – Gough and the others escaped with $7000 of gold from the Maryville robbery, but Hank Knott was captured. We have buried the gold in a remote spot in Gable Canyon, and now we will ride across the Red Mountains into the next county where we can lie low for the next few months. I have written down the name of the place where the gold is hidden using Hayley's code. The keyword is Hayley's nickname.

B B C E
H X U D
E S J E
F C C A

The new railroad from Maryville to Fort Bloomsburg was opened by Governor James Chichester III amid great celebrations on Tuesday afternoon. The Governor praised all those whose courage and determination had made "the railroad dream" come true. However, there was controversy in the air when railroad owner Sam "Turncoat" Hayley rose to make his inaugural speech. Many remember the trial five years ago when Hayley was accused of abetting the notorious outlaw... ...e. Although cleared, there is ...dence that Hayley was guilty

...der unease.
...s of arrests
...inger Tom
...showdown
...on Saloon
...the crime
...ed out of
...at sunset
...bouts are
...ions are
...sehoods
...utation
...in the

MELROSE'S PATENT GUNPOWDER

Hayley's message. Keyword: Mustang

```
M U S T A N G   M U S T
B Y X D Y F F   S S X P
C O N S I G N   M E N T

A N G M U S T A N G M
B Z P W X M R Y S K I
O F G O L D W I L L B

U S T A N G M U S T A
S E P I B G I   J F Y
E O N M A I L   T R A I

N G M U S T A N G G
W N W E E V K T C
N T O M O R R O W
```

Kate Jonson sets out in search of Ben Pierce's secret hideaway, deep in the wild Red Mountains. After three days struggling along steep mountain trails; she reaches her goal, a cave in Kutter's Canyon. Kate begins to search the cave, which is littered with packing cases, sticks of dynamite and broken bottles. In one corner, she spots an old bundle of sacks. Among them, she finds a collection of yellowed papers.

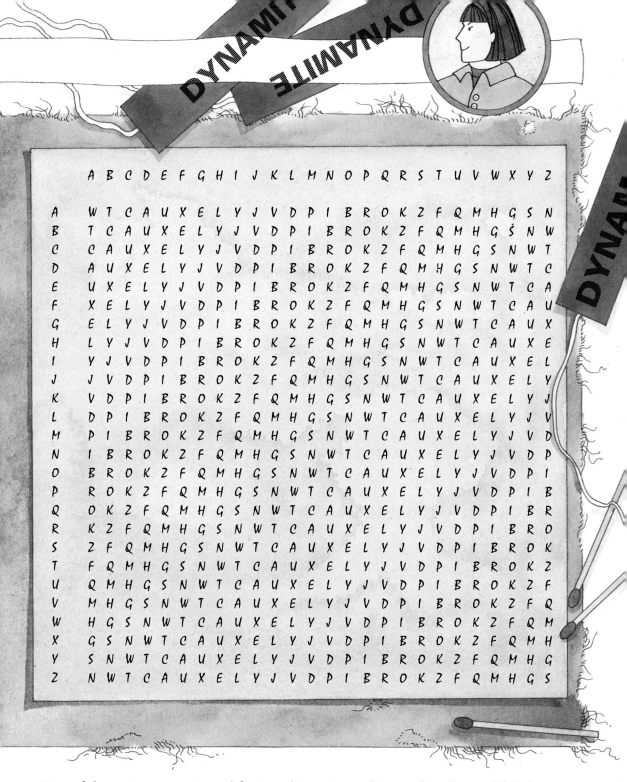

One of these is a page ripped from a diary. According to this, the scribbled letters on one of the scraps of paper form a coded message revealing where the gang hid the gold stolen from the Maryville mail train. If Kate can decipher the message, she will be able to name the hiding place and so fulfil her quest.

Where is the gold hidden?

Clocktower Communication

THIS PAINTING SHOWS THE GRAND PARADE AT THE MASQUE
4   5   6   3   3   2   1
10   7   11   11   8   8   7

JONES. THE MASQUE WAS HELD TO CELEBRATE THE
3   4   4   6   6
12   9   11   7   9

THE GRAND PARADE WAS LED BY THE KING HIMSELF. HE WAS
1   5   2   5   3   2   3   6
12   9   11   11   9   9 10   10

MARIANNE, MONSIEUR JEAN DE LA TOUBIERE, MADAME

To Roland Petanque,

I have discovered that Le Capitaine is planning to thwart the Montero Society's plot to steal the Sargasso Jewels. I have intercepted a message sent between two of Le Capitaine's allies, and this reveals his true identity. To decipher the message, you must take the 36 marked letters from the painting and write them on the fan. To do this, look at the two numbers beneath the first marked letter. Translate these numbers into musical notes, using the lanterns as a key. The two musical notes will enable you to pinpoint a single position on the fan. Write the first marked letter in this position, then continue in the same way until you have written all the marked letters onto the fan. Finally, read the message, which winds around the fan in a strange but predictable way.

Monsieur Thomas

Ben Harvey sets off for the town of Latoures. Four hundred years ago, Monsieur Thomas was ordered to leave communications to the Montero Society above the doorway of the clocktower in the town square. Could any messages still be there centuries later?

To his amazement, Ben finds a loose stone above the door, and pulls it away to reveal a small niche. Inside, he finds a tightly wrapped bundle. It contains a letter, a small painting and a fan. If Ben can decipher a message hidden in the painting and fan, he will finally discover the true identity of Le Capitaine.

OF LANTERNS, DEVISED BY THE INGENIOUS POET, ORLANDO

5	1	6	1	1	6	2
12	8	12	9	11	8	10

BIRTHDAY OF OUR ILLUSTRIOUS SOVEREIGN, HENRI XVIII.

1	4	5	5
10	12	10	8

FOLLOWED BY THE MARQUIS OF ST PIERRE, THE DUCHESS OF

4	4	3	2	2
8	7	7	12	7

ANNETTE DE GOUACHE AND MONSIEUR PAUL DELAMARE

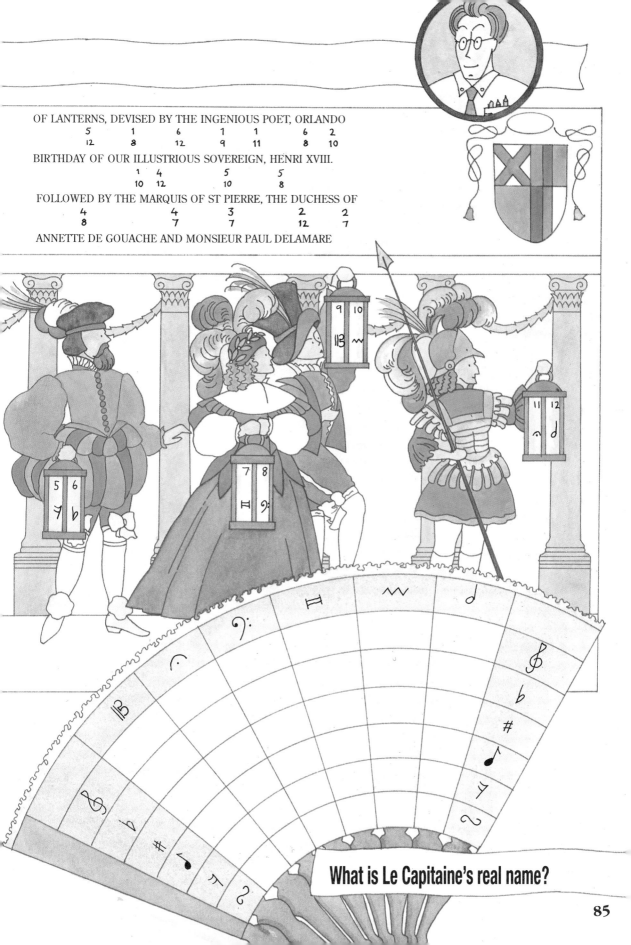

What is Le Capitaine's real name?

85

Pavilion Puzzle

To my devoted followers,
I have taken refuge in the Pavilion of
So Shong which lies just outside the
village of Tian Song. You must find your
way to the smallest room in the pavilion.
This is my secret chamber. Be warned:
two rooms in the building have been
boobytrapped by my faithful servant, Lo
Pin. With this letter, you will find a
coded plan of the pavilion. Use this to
find the safe route to my chamber. The
following explanations will help you make
sense of the plan.

Scale

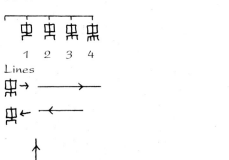

1 2 3 4

Lines

Room

)(Door

Rooms connected by door

Stairs connecting two rooms on
different floors

Booby trap. DO NOT ENTER

I trust that we shall meet again very
soon.
May you grow in wisdom and happiness,
Lo Chi

After a perilous journey across the
Chi Nen Mountains, Carrie Jones
reaches the village of Tian Song
where she retrieves Lo Chi's final set
of instructions. These consist of an
elaborate scroll, a picture of the
nearby Pavilion of So Shong and a
parchment covered with symbols.

According to the scroll, Lo Chi took
refuge in the pavilion, and his secret
chamber was the smallest room. The
symbols on the parchment form a
coded plan of the building. If Carrie
can make sense of the symbols, she
will be able to locate Lo Chi's
chamber. Then she will be able to
find a safe route to it and finally
retrieve the vital message left by
Thomas Hudson.

What is her route?

Pavilion of So Shong

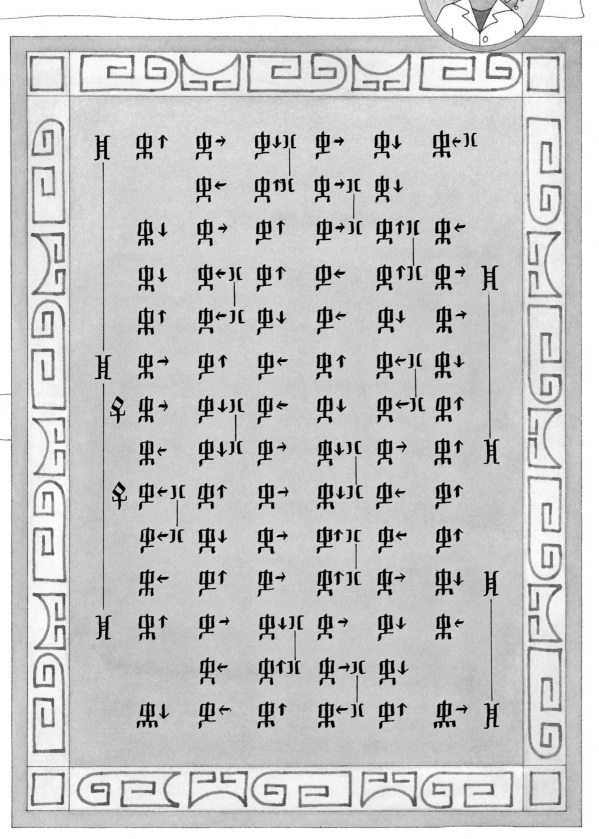

Thomas Hudson's Final Challenge

Carrie Jones rushes up the steps of the Rialto Hotel clutching the vital message that she retrieved from Lo Chi's secret chamber. She races to room 501 where Mat Smith, Kate Jonson, Sally Cameron and Ben Harvey have already assembled in time for Thomas Hudson's six o'clock deadline. As a clock strikes the hour, a mysterious figure in dark glasses walks slowly into the room. He places a sealed envelope on the table, then leaves.

To Mat Smith, Kate Jonson, Ben Harvey, Sally Cameron and Carrie Jones

Welcome back from your adventures! If you have all successfully completed your missions, you will now be ready to take on my final challenge. Using the two grids and the dial that you will find with this letter, you must decode the message which was left in Lo Chi's secret refuge. This reveals the location of the lost treasures of the ancient Bilongi civilization.

I encoded the name of the hiding place using a cipher which I devised myself:

First I wrote the name of the headquarters of the Red Panther Spy Ring across the top of the small grid, followed by the remaining letters of the alphabet. Using the grid, I then converted each letter of the treasures' location into two symbols by writing down the symbol at the beginning of the row, followed by the symbol at the top of the column.

Next I erased the letters from the grid, and across the top, I wrote the name of the mountain where Hapu built his stronghold, followed by the remaining letters of the alphabet. Then I used the grid to convert the real name of Le Capitaine into symbols.

I took the first symbol of the treasures' location and the first symbol of Le Capitaine's name and converted them into a number, using the large grid. I repeated this process until all the symbols were translated into numbers.

With the help of the dial, I converted the numbers into letters. For the first two numbers, I set the dial so that 1 represented the first letter of the name of the place where Pierce and his gang hid the loot from the Maryville mail train. For the second two numbers I set the dial so that 1 represented the second letter, and so on, until I reached the end.

If you can decode the message, you will be able to find the long lost treasures and embark on an exciting life of adventure. If you fail, then only obscurity beckons ...

Good luck,

Thomas Hudson.

Ripping open the envelope, the adventurers find a letter from Thomas Hudson. This tells them that the information they have uncovered holds the key to the vital message that Carrie retrieved. If they can decode the message, they will discover the location of the lost treasures of the Bilongi civilization. If not, the secret will remain hidden for ever.

Where are the lost treasures?

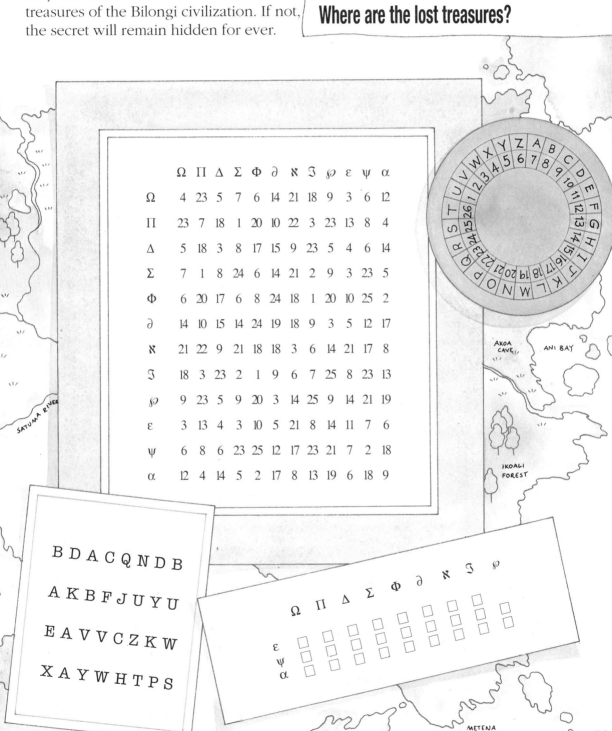

Clues

Pages 52-53

To find out which code has been used for the first message, work through the instructions for each code in reverse. By a process of trial and error, you will find out which code has been used. Decode the other messages in the same way.

Pages 54-55

The scrap of paper is the key to crack this message. Then just follow Pierce's instructions exactly. A message should soon start to appear.

Pages 56-57

Read Henri de la Motte's letter carefully. It does not matter which side of the playing cards you use!

Pages 58-59

As the word U is the only single letter word in the ancient Bilongi language, the letter U must correspond to the symbol ≋ on the parchment. Now look at the last word in the third line. The last letter of this word is U. How many six-letter words ending with U can you find in the list? You should now know which symbols correspond to T, E, O and N. From here, it should be quite easy to identify which symbols relate to the other English letters.

Pages 60-61

Treat this boardgame as a jigsaw puzzle. Start with the two cross shaped pieces. And remember – each piece can only be used once!

Pages 62-63

Start by trying to discover how each scrambler switch rearranges the symbols. Now assume that the first switch has been used to encode the message. What order would the symbols have been in originally? Try translating the reordered symbols into letters. Does a message start to appear? If not, try the other two scrambling orders.

Pages 64-65

Once you have discovered how the coding device works, it should be quite easy to rearrange the lines in the diary. Imagine sliding the symbol on the 'Coded Line' part of the ruler so that it is above the same symbol on the 'Original Line' section of the ruler.

Pages 66-67

Start by writing out the message without the numbers or symbols. You should then be able to fill in some of the spaces with the missing letters and consequently discover which three numbers or symbols have been used for each letter.

Pages 68-69

Start with the following two sentences:
'Adiki struck Oba'
'Adiki sailed away'.
The word 'Adiki' appears in both of these sentences. As the only symbol the sentences have in common is 朮, this must mean Adiki.

Pages 70-71

Follow the letter closely. Lo Chi's instructions are very clear, but it is a long process.

Pages 72-73

Work through the encoding instructions in reverse to uncover the original message. You will need to use all the papers on these pages.

Page 74

The size of the letters is the key to this puzzle. But you will need to fill in the large disk as well.

Page 75

Could the shapes on the picture have any connection with the shapes surrounding the letters on the counters?

Page 76-77

Translating the symbols is the easy part. Remember that the pattern above the painting shows how the pictograms have been encoded, so you will have to work from right to left to decode them.

Pages 78-79

Lo Chi has yet again written very clear instructions! Follow them exactly to reveal the message. Don't forget to reset the wheel as instructed.

Pages 80-81

Remember to draw a new grid for each keyword. Then just translate the numbers back into letters.

Pages 82-83

Knowing the keyword is crucial for deciphering this message. You will find it in the news clipping. Now look at Hayley's message. The coded letters are typewritten. Can you make sense of the letters that Pierce has added? The large grid will help.

Pages 84-85

Follow Monsieur Thomas's letter exactly. Once you have written all the letters on the fan, read off the message starting in the bottom right-hand corner.

Pages 86-87

Look carefully at the explanation on Lo Chi's scroll. It may be simpler than it seems. Squared paper will help you to draw the plan. You should be able to plot a route to the smallest room – and remember to look out for the booby traps.

Pages 88-89

Work through Thomas Hudson's encoding process in reverse to reveal where the treasures are hidden. You will only be able to solve this code if you already know the answers to the puzzles on pages 76-77, 80-81, 82-83 and 84-85. Remember to draw the grids exactly as instructed, and follow the code step by step. This puzzle is not easy!

Answers

Pages 52-53

By a process of trial and error, Mat discovers which code has been used for each telegram. Then he can figure out what they say. Here are the translated messages with punctuation added:

ALMARO EXPRESS: TO SEAGULL FROM EAGLE. YOU ARE INSTRUCTED TO TAKE COMMAND OF OPERATION DINGBAT.
(Code TL4: Oranges and Lemons)

ADESSA TELEGRAMS: TO ALBATROSS FROM FALCON. REPORT TO SEAGULL AT THE MINISTRY OF COUNTER ESPIONAGE IN BALAIKA CITY.
(Code TL1: Mustard and Cress)

QST: TO SEAGULL FROM MACAW. RED PANTHER AGENTS HAVE INFILTRATED THE ALBONI RESEARCH INSTITUTE.
(Code TL3: Lobster Pot)

SENDERO TELEGRAMS: TO EAGLE AND RAVEN FROM SEAGULL. CARRY OUT SURVEILLANCE OPERATION AT ALBONI RESEARCH INSTITUTE. IDENTIFY RED PANTHER INFILTRATORS.
(Code TL5: Deadly Nightshade)

HALVANIA TELEGRAMS: TO SEAGULL FROM FALCON. WE HAVE IDENTIFIED AND ARRESTED ALBONI INFILTRATORS BUT RED PANTHER IS PLANNING NEW OPERATION AT UNKNOWN LOCATION – POSSIBLY OTHER RESEARCH ESTABLISHMENT.
(Code TL6: Laughing Demons)

Pages 54-55

Following Pierce's instructions, Kate pieces together the following message:

JOE GOUGH WILL HOLD UP THE MARYVILLE MAIL TRAIN ON MAY 31ST. YOU WILL TRAVEL AS PASSENGERS ON THE TRAIN. WHEN IT REACHES THE KLONDIKE PASS, FORCE THE DRIVER TO STOP.

Pages 56-57

Ben works through Henri de la Motte's letter. He finds two symbols from the playing cards, then uses these as a reference for the diamond-shaped grid.

He discovers that the meeting was to take place at CHATEAU LOT.

Pages 58-59

Once she knows which symbol corresponds with each letter, Sally can easily translate the inscriptions. This is what they say:

ON MIDSUMMER DAY, THE GREAT HERO, HAPU, WAS BORN ON THE ISLAND OF TIKI. HIS MOTHER WAS KAIA, WHO KNEW THE MEANING OF DREAMS, AND HIS FATHER WAS OBA THE FISHERMAN.

Pages 60-61

With all the pieces in place, the board looks like this:

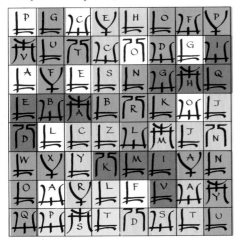

Reading the exposed letters in order, Carrie discovers that the next set of instructions was left at the PALACE OF GO.

Pages 62-63

Mat soon realizes that the symbols have been encoded using the third scrambling order. The other scrambling orders do not produce a message.

Working through the instructions on the blueprint in reverse, he uncovers the following message:

RADIO ROOM IS IN SCHOTT TOWER IN KAMAROV FOREST.

Pages 64-65

Using the coding device, Kate puts the lines of the diary entry into their original order. Then she reinstates the correct punctuation. This is what the diary says:

May 31st '84

I set off with Hank Knott at sunrise and we took up our positions in the Klondike Pass, waiting for the train to appear. At noon exactly, we heard the sound of a distant engine.

"Prepare to strike!" I yelled at Hank.

Minutes later the train came into view. We both knew the plan by heart. Danny Heape and Jake Sharp were aboard, and would force the driver to stop. At their signal, we'd attack.

The train screeched to a sudden halt. The plan was working! We rushed to the train, smashed open the doors of the mail van and grabbed the sacks of gold.

But at that moment I saw a column of horsemen riding in our direction. They were led by our old enemy, Marshal Jack Davenport! We raced back to our horses, staggering under the weight of the gold. Suddenly I saw Hank Knott stumble. Davenport rode straight at him. Hank scrambled to his feet, but seconds later he was in the marshal's clutches.

The rest of us leaped back onto our horses and galloped away from the scene. But Davenport was hot on our heels. We tore along the mountain trails, driving our horses as hard as we could, and at last we managed to outride our pursuers. We laid low until nightfall, then set out for the secret hideaway. But when we arrived, Pierce was waiting for us with bad news. Hank Knott had been taken to Fort Davenport and had betrayed us! He had even handed over details of the location of our hideaway. We buried the loot in a secret place, then fled into the next county.

Pages 66-67

Once Ben has discovered which numbers and symbols have been used for each letter, he can easily decode the message. The key is shown here:

A = 6, 4, &   O = 1, 3, *
E = ¿, 2, 9   U = ¶, §, 7
I = ¡, 5, 8

This is what the writing says:

As soon as the meeting opened, the Duke of Thierry announced that Le Capitaine had thwarted our activities for a third time. Five members of the Society were caught red handed during the attempt to steal the Orlando Diamonds and they are now rotting in the Carcelle prison. The Duke demanded that we discover the identity of Le Capitaine so that we can eliminate him once and for all. Immediately, Roland Petanque leaped to his feet announcing that he had hired a certain Monsieur Thomas to discover his true identity. Monsieur Thomas is one of the most cunning rogues in the whole kingdom. The Duke was pleased at the news and offered to reward Monsieur Thomas with five hundred francs if he succeeds.

Pages 68-69

By a process of deduction, Sally figures out the meaning of each of the ancient symbols. Then she translates the symbols on the snake into English.

Finally she puts the words into the right order, using the sentences on Anita Raia's notes as a model. This is what the inscriptions say:

THE EARTHQUAKE STRUCK TIKI.

THE ISLANDERS LEFT TIKI.

HAPU LED ONE GROUP.

KINJA LED ANOTHER GROUP.

HAPU SAILED TO GUANA.

Pages 70-71

Following Lo Chi's instructions, Carrie uncovers the following message:

GO TO THE PAGODA OF HO MIN XEN AND FIND THE KEEPER OF THE ROBES.

Pages 72-73

Working backward through the directions in the code book, Mat reveals the following message:

RED PANTHER HQ LOCATED. DETAILS SENT TO BUNKER IN SATROIKA.

Page 74

First, Kate fills in the missing numbers on the large disk. The completed disk is shown on the right.

Next she follows Pierce's directions to discover that the hideaway is in STOKER'S CAVERN. This is marked near the top of the map.

Page 75

Using the shapes on the disks as a key, Ben uncovers the following message:
CLOCKTOWER IN LATOURES, ABOVE THE DOORWAY.

Pages 76-77

Using the lists of symbols, Sally translates the pictograms into English. Then, examining the patterns at the top of the painting, she realizes that they have been rearranged in the following stages:

1. The symbols are written out in a spiral:

2. The vertical columns are reordered:

3. The symbols are read off in a zigzag:

Sally works through this process in reverse to reveal the following message:

THE GREAT HAPU BUILT HIS STRONGHOLD ON KILUMENA MOUNTAIN, WHICH IS LOWER THAN LANKALI MOUNTAIN. INKURA MOUNTAIN HAS NO SNAKES. MANIKI MOUNTAIN HAS NO RIVER.

Pages 78-79

Using the yellow piece of paper, Carrie finds the following symbols on the large chart:

   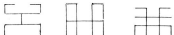

She then uses the code wheel to translate them into letters. She discovers that Lo Chi's refuge was in the village of TIAN SONG.

Pages 80-81

First of all, Mat finds the four keywords, which are all road names on the map. They are:

1. SMETYNA
2. DYMITRA
3. YVESTIA
4. RADIKOV

Now he can draw the grids and decipher the numbers to reveal the following message:

RED PANTHER HQ IS AT TSAR CLUB.

Pages 82-83

From the news clipping, Kate learns that Hayley's nickname was 'Turncoat'.

Using this as the keyword, she decodes Pierce's message. She discovers that the gold was hidden at the VULTURES' NEST ROCK.

Pages 84-85

First, Ben writes the marked letters onto the fan. Then he reads off the message starting in the bottom right-hand corner. The completed fan is shown here.

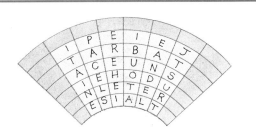

The message reads:

TRUST JEAN DE LA TOUBIERE.
HE IS LE CAPITAINE.

Pages 86-87

Following the instructions in Lo Chi's letter, Carrie draws the plan of the Pagoda shown here.

She knows that Lo Chi's chamber was the smallest room in the building. This is marked with a cross. To reach it, Carrie must go through the numbered rooms in order. Rooms connected by stairs are joined with a curved line.

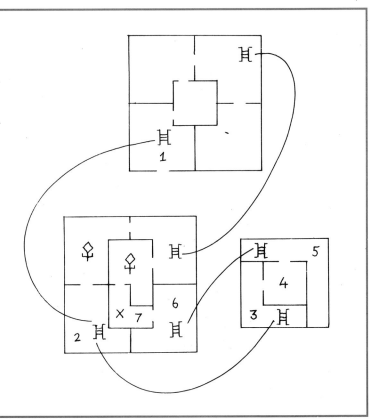

Pages 88-89

Working through Thomas Hudson's instructions in reverse, the five adventurers discover that the Bilongi treasures are hidden in ANI CAVE IN AKOA BAY. This is shown on the right of the map.

LOGIC PUZZLES

Mark Fowler

Illustrated by
Radhi Parekh

Designed by
Radhi Parekh and Sarah Dixon

Edited by
Sarah Dixon

Contents

Before You Start

Baffling brainteasers, cryptic sequences, strange conundrums, complex board games . . . all these and more lie in wait on the pages ahead. Every puzzle can be solved by logical deduction. Some are moderately tricky, while others could prove fiendishly difficult.

Look carefully at the documents and illustrations which accompany each puzzle. They contain all the information you need to find the solution. If you get stuck, turn to pages 138-140 for clues and hints on how to tackle the puzzles. You will find the answers on pages 141-144.

You can pick out a puzzle at random to solve, if you dare. But if you tackle them in order, you will discover several stories emerging, with a recurring cast of characters. Each story can be identified by its emblem and its heading, as shown on this double page.

There is more to these five stories than meets the eye, for buried in their midst is the strange tale of the seven lost statues of Alfresco. On page 140 there are hints to set you on the trail of these statues, but it is up to you to unravel the book's central mystery and locate their final hiding place.

Skarpa the Bold and the Weather Charm of Wailen Valla

Skarpa the Bold is a heroic adventurer from the northern land of Maelstrom. During the Dismal Age of Turmoil and Strife, raiders attack Maelstrom's shores and carry off a ship's figurehead known as the Weather Charm of Wailen Valla. Skarpa vows to recover the figurehead, for only this protects Maelstrom from the fierce storms which rage across the Northern Seas. His adventures have been pieced together using a selection of objects found inside an ancient longboat.

Carilla di Galliard and the Statue of the Cantador

Carilla di Galliard lives in Madrigola, a kingdom many miles south of Maelstrom, during the Merry Age of Minstrels. Almost all Madrigolans are fine musicians, but Carilla cannot sing or play a note. She is searching for a statue called the Cantador, for legend says that whoever finds this magic figure will become a great musician. Four tapestries from the Grand Palace of Madrigola illustrate Carilla's quest.

Peg Traherne and the Search for Obadiah Walrus

Peg Traherne is a secret agent living in the land of Wayward during the Swashbuckling Age of Buccaneers. Her latest mission is to track down Obadiah Walrus, the missing leader of a recently-formed group called the Society of Alfresco. The details of Peg's adventures are revealed in a bundle of papers found inside an old pirate fort in the distant Heliotropic Islands.

Percival Sharpe and the Faymus Treasures

One hundred and fifty years later, four valuable treasures are stolen from Faymus Towers, a large house in the middle of Cragge, Wayward's northernmost village. Renowned sleuth Percival Sharpe is called in to track down the thieves and recover the stolen treasures. Percival's investigations have been reconstructed using a selection of exhibits from Wayward Museum.

Freya de Fresque and the Alfrescan Casket

At the beginning of the Modern Age, the Society of Alfresco sends Madrigola's leading explorer, Freya de Fresque, to the eastern land of Magenta. Freya's mission is to retrieve the mysterious Alfrescan Casket from a secret hiding place. Her journey across Magenta is charted for the first time using the contents of an old chest from the society's headquarters.

The Seven Statues

The seven mysterious statues come from the island of Alfresco, and depict the gods of food, drink, jests, acrobatics, dance, poetry and music. Over a thousand years ago, they were stolen by a band of raiders called the Cafelors and ever since then the island has been stricken by disaster. The Society of Alfresco has vowed to find the statues and return them to Alfresco, in the belief that this will restore the island's good fortune. So far, the evil descendents of the Cafelors have thwarted them in their worthy quest, but now there is a chance to ensure the society's success for these pages contain all the information needed to track down the seven statues and bring in a new Alfrescan golden age.

Midnight Rendezvous

Acting on the instructions of the Society of Alfresco, secret agent Peg Traherne rides to an old castle on Wayward Moor. Here she must meet a contact who has information that will help her in her mission to find the society's missing leader, Obadiah Walrus. She knows that the castle is surrounded by members of the sinister Cafelors organization and her contact is trapped inside. One of the castle's entrances will be left unguarded after midnight. Peg must find the safe door so that she can meet her contact.

Which is the safe entrance?

Jonson not Ø - guarding either the Old Keep or the East Tower.

The Society of Alfresco
October 13th

The Bell Tower is not guarded by Hook or Morgrim

To Agent Traherne,
You must go to Castle Cloud on Wayward Moor to meet a contact who has information vital to your mission. The castle has been surrounded by seven members of a sinister organization called the Cafelors. They are guarding all seven entrances and your contact is trapped inside. However, one entrance will be left unguarded between midnight and one o'clock tonight, when a guard called Morgrim must contact his cronies in Marshby. You must discover which entrance Morgrim is guarding and slip inside the castle during his absence.

Morgrim's fellow guards are called Shark, Jonson, Graves, Smythe, Clipper and Hook. The seven are also known by the following symbols: Ω, Ψ, Э, Ø, Σ, ∇ and ∧. We don't know who has which symbol, except for Smythe who is Σ. Morgrim is not Э, ∇, or Ø, and Э is not Shark, Jonson, or Graves. Ø is not guarding the entrance to the Bell Tower, the Great Hall, or the North Tower, and neither Ψ nor ∇ are guarding the Old Keep.

We enclose the two lockets and four views of the castle. These contain all the other information we have been able to gather.

Good luck

The Ghost Tower is not guarded by ∇ or Э

Hook - not Ψ or Ø - not guarding the East Tower or the Great Hall

Ω is guarding the East Tower

Cloud - North View

Castle Cloud - East

The Old Keep is not guarded by Clipper, Hook or Shark

The Great Hall

Graves is guarding the North Tower

The South Tower is not guarded by ∇, Э or ∧

Castle Cloud - South View

Castle Cloud - West View

The Secret of the Symbols

At a great ceremony held on the feast day of the four-headed dragon, Skarpa the Bold vows to recover the stolen Weather Charm of Wailen Valla. Before he can begin his search, Skarpa has to seek the advice of Fjor, the wise enchanter. Fjor lives in the Hall of Fire and Ice across Maelstrom's hazardous northern wastes. With the help of this strange table of symbols, Skarpa must discover which five perilous places he will encounter on his way to the enchanter's hall.

What are the five places?

This chart shows the symbols carved on the great stones that stand in the perilous places of the northern land of Maelstrom. To discover which of these places you must pass to reach the hall of fire and ice, choose one symbol from each of the five central columns. Mark this with a cross each time it is repeated down that column. If you choose wisely, only one of the five symbols will be marked in each row. The location of each stone is written next to its symbol on each side of the chart.

A Cryptic Sequence

At the beginning of his investigation into the theft of the Faymus Treasures, renowned sleuth Percival Sharpe is sent a mysterious package. It contains a curious dial, a pictorial map covered with cryptic emblems and a letter addressed to one of the thieves. On reading the letter, Percival realizes that he can use the map and the dial to discover where the villains were staying on the night of the crime.

Where were they staying?

To: ⧆

Tomorrow you will receive a package from headquarters. It contains a dial and a map showing all the buildings in the village of Cragge. Each building on the map has an emblem that is divided into five sections. Each section contains a shape and a symbol. The symbols represent numbers, as shown on the dial.

Five of the emblems form a sequence. The first, second and fifth emblems of the sequence are:

You must identify the third and fourth emblems. To do this, first translate the symbols into numbers and then look for five number sequences which run from the first emblem to the fifth. The first sequence links the numbers in the triangles; the second links the numbers in the diamonds; the third links the numbers in the squares; the fourth links the numbers in the circles and the fifth links the numbers in the pentagons. Finally, the shapes themselves move around the five emblems in a strange but predictable way.

The building marked with the fourth emblem is your base for Operaion Faymus. On December 30th, you must make contact with Ω at the base. On the night of the 31st, you and Ω will break into Faymus Towers and steal the Faymus Treasures, then return to the base to await further orders.

The dial sent to ⧆

A PICTORIAL MAP
of the village of
CRAGGE

The Mummers' Advice

This tapestry shows the five Mummers of Marcato, the most confusing band of performers in all Madrigola. One of the Mummers speaks the truth all the time. One tells nothing but lies. The other three tell a mixture of truth and lies.

When asked how to find the statue, I say: "You must take the road to the town of Tabor."

You say no such thing

You must take the road

to the city of Mandolin

Indeed you must take

the road to Mandolin

At the crossroads, you must go to Castle Gargoylia

You must go to the

Castle of Arc

You must not go to Castle Gargoylia

You must go to castle Gargoylia

You must head either to

Tabor or to Mandolin

I always tell a mixture

of truth and lies

That is not true

If the bear is always truthful

the juggler tells nothing but lies

That is false

At the castle you must find the sage

The Drummer

always tells the truth

The piper tells nothing but lies

You must find the pageboy

You must find the cook

THE STATUE OF THE GOD OF ACROBATICS WAS MADE IN AGONDA VILLAGE

Carilla di Galliard sets off across the land of Madrigola in search of the statue of the Cantador. At a fork in the road she meets a band of entertainers called the Mummers of Marcato who offer her advice. This tapestry shows their confusing suggestions. Carilla must find out which of their statements are truthful and so discover what to do next.

What should Carilla do?

The Route to the Amethyst Cave

Explorer Freya de Fresque sets off for the distant land of Magenta to retrieve the valuable Alfrescan Casket on behalf of the Society of Alfresco. At the Magentan port of Lapis Lazuli she collects a battered envelope containing a mysterious Magentan chart and an old letter.

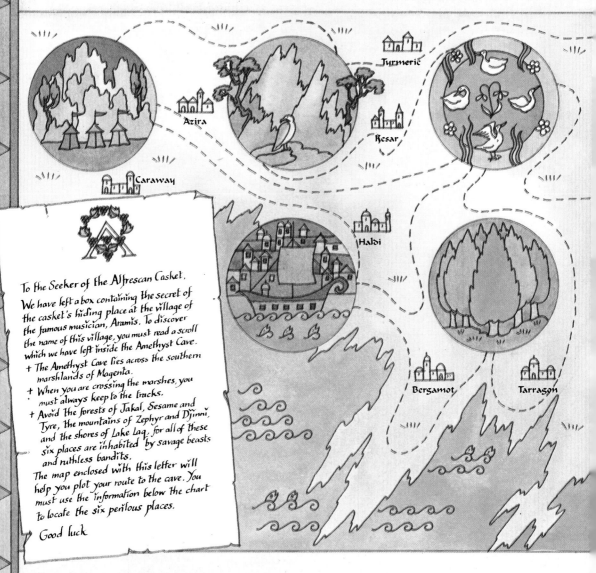

Turmeric

Azira

Kesar

Caraway

Haldi

Bergamot

Tarragon

To the Seeker of the Alfrescan Casket,

We have left a box containing the secret of the casket's hiding place at the village of the famous musician, Aramis. To discover the name of this village, you must read a scroll which we have left inside the Amethyst Cave.

+ The Amethyst Cave lies across the southern marshlands of Magenta.

+ When you are crossing the marshes, you must always keep to the tracks.

+ Avoid the forests of Jakal, Sesame and Tyre, the mountains of Zephyr and Djinni, and the shores of Lake Laq, for all of these six places are inhabited by savage beasts and ruthless bandits.

The map enclosed with this letter will help you plot your route to the cave. You must use the information below the chart to locate the six perilous places.

Good luck

This chart of the Southern Marshlands of Magenta shows the tracks that link the region's mountain ranges, forests and lakes with the Amethyst Cave and the port of Lapis Lazuli.
It takes five days to walk along each path shown on the map
The Forest of Sesame is five days' walk from Lake Laq
Lake Tirin is five days' walk from the Forest of Tyre
The Forest of Okra is five days' walk from the Mountains of Nadir
The Djinni Mountains are five days' walk from Lake Aral

According to the letter, a piece of vital information about the casket's hiding place has been left in the Amethyst Cave far across Magenta's treacherous southern marshes. Using the map, Freya must plot a safe route to the cave avoiding this region's six most hazardous landmarks.

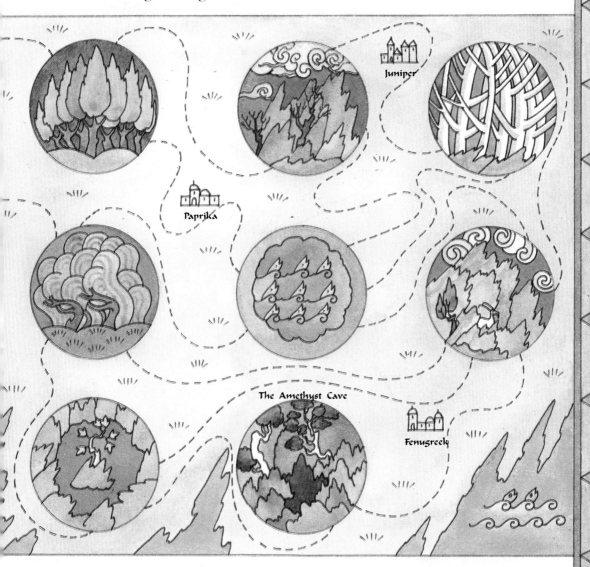

The Zephyr Mountains are more than five days' walk from the Forest of Sesame
Lake Laq is more than five days' walk from the Djinni Mountains
The Forest of Tyre is more than five days' walk from the port of Lapis Lazuli
Lake Laq is more than five days' walk from the Mountains of Nadir
The Forest of Tyre is more than five days' walk from Lake Aral
The Mountains of Nadir are more than five days' walk from the Forest of Tyre
The Cyan Mountains are more than five days' walk from the Forest of Jakal

What is Freya's route?

The Enigma of the Runik Isles

on this my cunning chart i show the six islands of the runik people. on each island there are six villages, and each village has been given a secret sign. for each village, i show four signs but only one sign is the village's true sign and the other three are false signs. no two villages on the same island share the same true sign. no village that shares its flag with any other village in the runik isles will share that other village's true sign.

According to Fjor the Enchanter, the Weather Charm of Wailen Valla was stolen by the Warriors of the Whirlwind. These fearsome raiders come from the Isle of Doom Laiden, far across the windswept Western Seas. The only person who can guide Skarpa to this island is an explorer called Seega the Seafarer who lives in the village of Kamott in the Runik Isles.

To help Skarpa find Seega's village, the enchanter presents him with a talisman and a map of the Runik Isles. None of the villages is named on this map. Instead each one is identified by a flag and a symbol. Kamott's flag and symbol are carved on the talisman, but can Skarpa locate the village on the map?

Which village is Kamott?

The Riddle of the Knights

Carilla's search for the statue of the Cantador leads her to the Great Tournament of Madrigola. Here she learns that she must seek the help of Sir Jules Hautboys. Sir Jules is one of ten knights competing in the tournament. This tapestry shows the knights and all the details that Carilla can discover about them. By piecing this information together, she is able to identify Sir Jules.

This is the horse of Sir Gawain

The horse of Sir Caspar

The owner of this shield has a horse with red reins

This valiant knight has a horse with red reins

Sir Emilio

Sir Almeric and his horse

The owner of this shield has a horse with red reins

This scene shows the ten knights who fought at the great tournament of Madrigola, together with their horses and shields. Sir Gerard's horse has a great plume. The shields of Sir Almeric and Sir Jules are different shapes, but they have the same design. Sir Gerard's shield has a cross. Sir Sigismund has a black horse while the horse of Sir Balthus is white as snow. The champion of the joust is Sir Fernando the Flamboyant.

The owner of this shield rides a white horse

Sir Harold

Which knight is Sir Jules?

The Albatross Conundrum

At the castle, secret agent Peg Traherne learns that she must go to a ship called the Albatross, anchored at the port of Great Rigging. The Society of Alfresco's missing leader, Obadiah Walrus, was a passenger aboard this ship on its last voyage across the Southern Seas, but he never reached his destination. The details of his fate are recorded in the log book of the Albatross. This has been hidden in a barrel on the deck commanded by Lieutenant Draconio. Using an old plan of the ship and a mysterious letter, Peg must identify Draconio's deck.

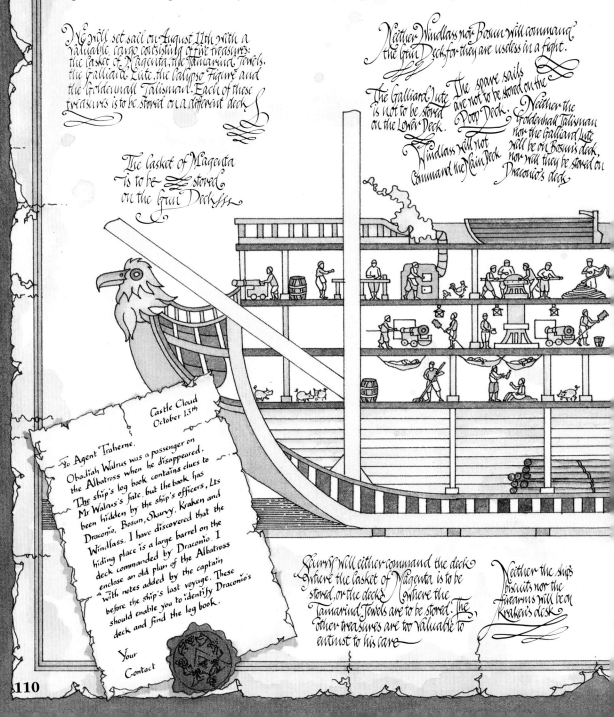

We will set sail on August 11th with a valuable cargo consisting of five treasures: the Casket of Magenta, the Tamarind Jewels, the Galliard Lute, the Calypso Figure and the Goldenhall Talisman. Each of these treasures is to be stored on a different deck.

The Casket of Magenta is to be stored on the Gun Deck.

Neither Windlass nor Bosun will command the Gun Deck, for they are useless in a fight.

The Galliard Lute is not to be stored on the Lower Deck.

The spare sails are not to be stored on the Poop Deck.

Neither the Goldenhall Talisman nor the Galliard Lute will be on Bosun's deck, nor will they be stored on Draconio's deck.

Windlass will not command the Main Deck.

Castle Cloud
October 13th

To Agent Traherne,

Obadiah Walrus was a passenger on the Albatross when he disappeared. The ship's log book contains clues to Mr Walrus's fate, but the book has been hidden by the ship's officers, Lts Draconio, Bosun, Skurvy, Kraken and Windlass. I have discovered that the hiding place is a large barrel on the deck commanded by Draconio. I enclose an old plan of the Albatross with notes added by the captain before the ship's last voyage. These should enable you to identify Draconio's deck and find the log book.

Your
Contact

Skurvy will either command the deck where the Casket of Magenta is to be stored, or the deck where the Tamarind Jewels are to be stored. The other treasures are too valuable to entrust to his care.

Neither the ship's biscuits nor the firearms will be on Kraken's deck.

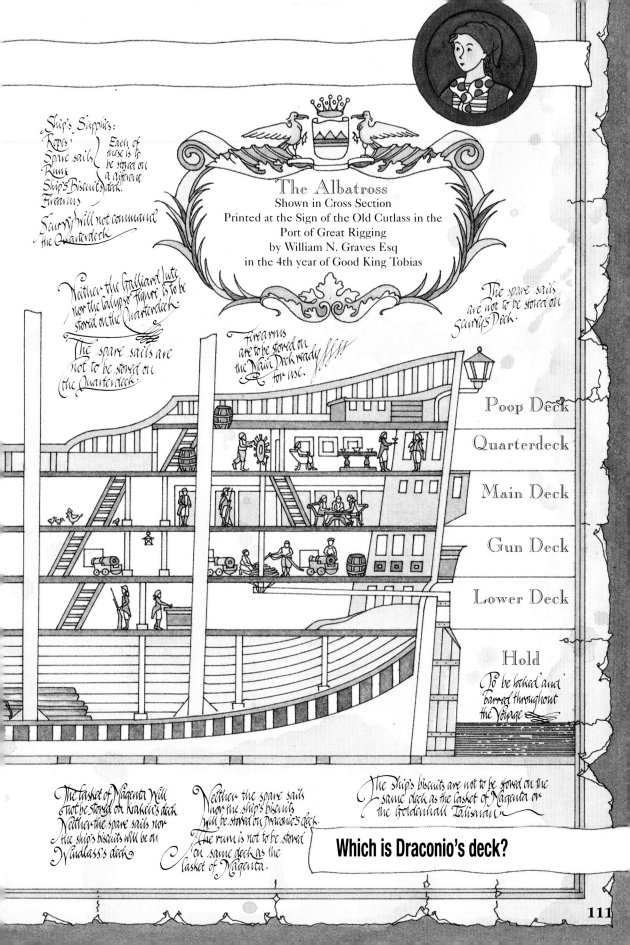

Ship's Supplies:
'Ropes'
Spare sails
Rum
Ship's Biscuits
Firearms

Each of these is to be stored on a different deck.

Scurvy will not command the Quarterdeck

The Albatross
Shown in Cross Section
Printed at the Sign of the Old Cutlass in the
Port of Great Rigging
by William N. Graves Esq
in the 4th year of Good King Tobias

Neither the Galliard lute nor the Calypso figure is to be stored on the Quarterdeck

The spare sails are not to be stored on the Quarterdeck

Firearms are to be stored on the Main Deck ready for use.

The spare sails are not to be stored on Scurvy's Deck.

Poop Deck

Quarterdeck

Main Deck

Gun Deck

Lower Deck

Hold
To be locked and barred throughout the voyage

The casket of Magenta will not be stored on Kraken's deck. Neither the spare sails nor the ship's biscuits will be on Windlass's deck.

Neither the spare sails nor the ship's biscuits will be stored on Draconio's deck. The rum is not to be stored on same deck as the casket of Magenta.

The ship's biscuits are not to be stored on the same deck as the casket of Magenta or the Goldenhall Talisman.

Which is Draconio's deck?

111

Ten Suspects

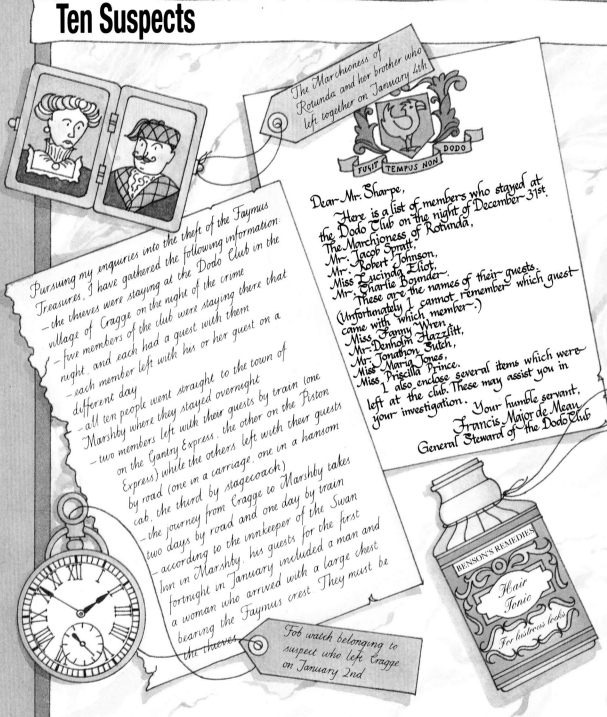

The Marchioness of Rotunda and her brother who left together on January 4th

FUGIT TEMPUS NON DODO

Dear Mr. Sharpe,
    Here is a list of members who stayed at the Dodo Club on the night of December 31st.
The Marchioness of Rotunda,
Mr. Jacob Spratt,
Mr. Robert Johnson,
Miss Lucinda Eliot,
Mr. Charlie Bounder.
    These are the names of their guests. (Unfortunately I cannot remember which guest came with which member.)
Miss Fanny Wren,
Mr. Denholm Hazzlitt,
Mr. Jonathon Sutch,
Miss Maria Jones,
Miss Priscilla Prince.
    I also enclose several items which were left at the club. These may assist you in your investigation.
        Your humble servant,
        Francis Major de Mean,
        General Steward of the Dodo Club

Pursuing my enquiries into the theft of the Faymus Treasures, I have gathered the following information:
– the thieves were staying at the Dodo Club in the village of Cragge on the night of the crime
– five members of the club were staying there that night, and each had a guest with them
– each member left with his or her guest on a different day
– all ten people went straight to the town of Marshby where they stayed overnight
– two members left with their guests by train (one on the Gantry Express, the other on the Piston Express) while the others left with their guests by road (one in a carriage, one in a hansom cab, the third by stagecoach)
– the journey from Cragge to Marshby takes two days by road and one day by train
– according to the innkeeper of the Swan Inn in Marshby, his guests for the first fortnight in January included a man and a woman who arrived with a large chest bearing the Faymus crest. They must be the thieves.

Fob watch belonging to suspect who left Cragge on January 2nd

BENSON'S REMEDIES
Hair Tonic
For lustrous locks

Hot on the trail of the thieves of the Faymus treasures, Percival Sharpe arrives at the headquarters of the exclusive Dodo Club. He knows that the thieves were among ten people staying at the club on the night of the crime. With the help of the club's steward, he gathers a bewildering assortment of information about the movements of all ten people. Once all the facts are pieced together, he will know which of the ten are the thieves.

This letter arrived on January 2nd, the day after Mr Sutch left Cragge

J. Sutch Esq.,
c/o The Dodo Club,
Cragge Village

Opera glasses belonging to suspect who left Cragge on January 7th

The owner of this bottle left Cragge on January 5th

Est. 1851

Harcourt's Hansom Cabs

Miss Fanny Wren left in a hansom, but not with Mr Charlie Bounder. Bounder left three days before Miss Prince.

The suspects who went by the Piston Express did not leave on January 1st

FLOODS STRIKE MARSHBY

The historic town of Marshby was flooded on January 6th during a freak storm. Fifteen buildings had to be evacuated, including the 400 year-old Swan Inn. "Our rooms were knee deep in water," said the inn's proprietor, Mr Jeremiah Drake. "We could not reopen for business until January 8th."

MARCHIONESS BECOMES GRAND DODO

At a lavish ceremony at the Dodo Club on December 31st, the Marchioness of Rotunda was invested as the new Grand Dodo. Club member Robert Johnson gave an eloquent speech in which he described the Marchioness as "probably the greatest Dodo of all time".

NOTICE OF AUCTION

On February 1st an auction will take place at Nether Marshby Manor, home of the late Colonel Windermere. Among the items for sale is a plant stand fashioned from a statue known as the Acrostik Acrobat, which Colonel Windermere acquired during a visit to the land of Magenta.

G G T C

THE GREAT GANTRY TRAIN COMPANY proudly announces the opening of a railway line between the village of CRAGGE and the historic town of MARSHBY.

Gone are the days when you had to wait for the once weekly stagecoach. Now you have a choice of two trains a week. Both the GANTRY EXPRESS and the PISTON EXPRESS race through the countryside at more than twice the speed of the stagecoach. If you choose to take the PISTON EXPRESS from CRAGGE to MARSHBY, you will leave one day after the stagecoach but arrive at your destination at exactly the same time. What is more, both our trains are furnished to the highest standards of luxury and elegance.

A SUPERLATIVE EXPERIENCE!

Historic Marshby

Jacob Spratt Esq

This suspect left on the Gantry Express, arriving at Marshby three days after Mr R. Johnson

Who are the thieves?

The Riddle of the Musicians

In the 23rd year of the reign of King Samerkland the Wise, nine visitors from the Society of Alfresco came to Magenta in search of the lost statue of Wine and Wassail. The ten musicians of Magenta held a concert to entertain the visitors.
This painting shows the musicians playing a stirring piece of music called the Kantador. The names of their villages are written on their music stands.
Lalik is at Izarin's left side.
Balbek is in the pavilion with the red flag.
Sulah is at Balbek's side.

Aramis and Faron are in the same pavilion, but are not next to one another.
If Korabeth wears a white turban, Balbek wears one too.
Qat is either in the front row of the pavilion with the red flag or in the front row of the pavilion with the yellow flag.
If Haliah has a cloak, Aramis has one too.
Haliah is at Raban's side
Aramis wears a white turban, but only if Lalik wears a cloak.
Korabeth is in the pavilion with the yellow flag.

Inside the Amethyst Cave, Freya de Fresque finds a painting from an old Magentan manuscript. This depicts a gathering of ten musicians from the villages of Magenta. Freya knows that she must go to the village of the musician called Aramis. Here she must collect a box which contains the secret of the Alfrescan Casket's hiding place. To discover the name of this village, she has to find out which of the ten players in the painting is Aramis.

What is the name of the village?

The Pirates' Island

Secret agent Peg Traherne hides aboard the Albatross before it sets sail on its next voyage. From the ship's log book, she has discovered that Obadiah Walrus was captured by a ruthless band of pirates from one of the seven Heliotropic Islands. Once the Albatross reaches these islands, Peg plans to swim ashore to rescue the pirates' hapless captive. But first she must identify their island using a poster and an earlier entry in the log book.

The Runaatongs of the Heliotropic Islands

1 Short-Haired Runaatong *(found on either Jaspar or Salamander Isle)*
2 Silver Runaatong *(found on Jaspar, Solferino or Eastern Islands)*
3 Klamorus Runaatong *(found on Corallina Island)*
4 Bouncing Runaatong
5 Howling Runaatong *(not on Jaspar Island)*
6 Rufus Runaatong
7 Long-Tailed Runaatong *(not on Cinnabar Island)*

WANTED FOR PIRA[TES]

A reward of ONE THOUSAND GOLD SOVEREIGN[S] awaits the person who can bring the dastardly, despic[able] and devious pirates of the Southern Seas to justice. T[hese] ruthless freebooters operate from the Fort of Skulls, [a] stronghold built on the ruins of an ancient palace on [one] one of the Heliotropic Isles.

Barebones Jake

Buccaneer Bess

THE STATUE OF THE GOD OF DANKE · WAS MADE IN ALUNA VILLAGE ·

14th February

During the great storm, the ship suffered terrible damage and for three weeks we drifted until at da[wn] this morning we sighted the Heliotropic Islands.

As the crew celebrated, I set out to explore the islands with Isaac Skew, the naturalist. We attempted to identify the islands, but this proved a difficult task. All seven islands are covered with dense jungle, but each has a distinguishing landmark. The first, which I identified as Solferino, has a grumbling volcano, while the second has vast mango groves. We found a hermitage on the fifth. The interior of the sixth is largely swamp, and the seventh has strange standing stones. From old sailors tales, I knew that neither the palace nor the tower were on Jaspar Island, and that neither the swamps nor the mango groves are not on Cinnabar Island, also remembered that the standing stones are not on Eastern Island.

Jaspar Island, the Isle of Parakeets or Eastern Island.

Isaac Skew told me that the Heliotropics are noted for their curious monkey-like creatures called Runaatongs, and that each island is home to a different species. With the help of Mr Skew's natural history book, we attempted to identify the Runaatongs that we glimpsed among the jungle foliage. We spotted a Bouncing Runaatong on the island with the palace. The runaatong that we saw on the isle of the swamps was not the Rufus or the Silver. The runaatong on the isle with the mango groves was not the Silver or the Howling. According to Mr. Skew, if the Long-Tailed lives on Eastern Island, the Rufus will not be on the island with standing stones; and if the tower is on the Isle of Parakeets, the Long-Tailed will not be on the island with the mango groves.

21st June

It is over four months since we left the Heliotropics, and at last we have reached the Isle of Alfresco. Fierce winds whip its shores, grey clouds shroud its hills. It is indeed a gloomy and desolate place.

Not on an island inhabited by runaatongs with spots.

Not on Eastern or Jaspar islands, or the Isle of Parakeets.

Hermitage of Marabout

Corallina Isle

Cinnabar

Eastern Island

Solferino

Jasper Island

Which is the pirates' island?

The Stone of Doom Laiden

The isle of lilla vaga. This island was not raided in the year of the midnight sun or the year of the storms. The year of the storms was not the year when the isle of loki was raided.

Knutt the fearsome. This warlord did not raid the isle of alfresco. He is not the owner of the south fort. He did not carry out his raid in the year of the mighty seamonster.

Gunhilde the ruthless. This warlord carried out a violent raid in the year of the great curse.

The isle of alfresco. This island was not raided in the year of the storms or the year of the great curse. It is a barren place and there was little to take back to the raider's stronghold, which is not the fort of blackstone.

Erik the mighty. This warlord is not the owner of the north fort or the fort of the dragonstone. Neither he nor harold the hardy carried out their raid in the year of the midnight sun.

Accompanied by Seega the Seafarer, Skarpa the Bold crosses the stormy Western Seas to the Isle of Doom Laiden. This island is the home of the Warriors of the Whirlwind, the fearsome band of raiders who stole the Weather Charm of Wailen Valla. According to Seega, they are led by five ruthless warlords. Each year, a different warlord takes command of the warriors and carries out a raid on a different land.

THE YEAR OF THE HEROIC SEA VOYAGE. THE SPOILS FROM THE PLACE RAIDED IN THIS YEAR (NOT THE ISLE OF VIDAR) WERE TAKEN TO THE FORT OF HIGH TOWERS, THE NORTH FORT OR THE FORT OF THE DRAGONSTONE.

SOMBRIK THE PROUD. THIS WARLORD IS NOT THE OWNER OF THE SOUTH FORT. HE DID NOT RAID THE ISLE OF ALFRESCO.

THE YEAR OF THE MIGHTY SEAMONSTER. IN THIS YEAR THE SPOILS OF A GREAT RAID WERE TAKEN TO THE NORTH FORT.

THE FORT OF HIGH TOWERS. THE SPOILS FROM THE ISLE OF VIDAR WERE TAKEN TO THIS FORT, BUT NOT BY GUNHILDE THE RUTHLESS OR SOMBRIK THE PROUD.

THE LAND OF MAELSTROM. THIS LAND WAS NOT RAIDED BY HAROLD THE HARDY OR SOMBRIK THE PROUD. THE SPOILS WERE NOT TAKEN TO THE SOUTH FORT OR THE FORT OF BLACKSTONE.

Each warlord lives with their warriors in a great fort on Doom Laiden. Skarpa suspects that the Weather Charm is hidden in the fort of the warlord who led the raid on Maelstrom. To identify this fort, Skarpa must piece together the inscriptions on a great stone that the vain warlords have erected on the island's shore to celebrate their most recent adventures.

Which fort should Skarpa search?

The Riddle of the Ten Towers

Sir Jules Hautboys sends Carilla to the Plains of Pavanne to find Aurora the Guardian of Secrets, for only she knows the fate of the statue of the Cantador. The Guardian lives in one of the ten towers on the plains, while the other nine are inhabited by the evil Lords of Lamotte. Carilla must locate the Guardian's tower using Sir Jules's descriptions. The towers are shown on this tapestry together with the knight's information.

Which is the Guardian's tower?

Here are the ten towers of the Plains of Pavanne
The Tower of Belle is across the river from the Tower of Torment
The Tower of Rigadoon is across the river from the Tower of Four Winds, but only if the Tower of Rigadoon stands on a hilltop
The Tower of Bay has a flag with an eagle
The Tower of Four Winds is across the river from the Tower of Torment, but only if the Tower of Four Winds has a pointed doorway
The Tower of Four Winds has a flag with a cross

The Tower of Rooks is on an island, but not if the Tower of Four Winds has a pointed doorway
The Tower of Four Winds has a flag with a lion, but only if the Tower of Sighs is surrounded by trees
The Tower of the Guardian is on the same side of the river as the Tower of Eagles, but not if the Tower of Bay has a flag with a lion
The Tower of the Sighs has more turrets than the Tower of Bay
The Tower of Eagles has fewer turrets than the Tower of the Guardian
The Tower of High Dudgeon has fewer turrets than the Tower of Eagles
The Tower of Belle stands on a hilltop

The Secret Handovers

After extensive inquiries, Percival Sharpe discovers that the thieves have left the country on a steamer belonging to the Kraken Shipping Company. At the company's ticket office at the port of Great Rigging, Percival is surprised to find a large parcel addressed to him. This contains a letter from an anonymous informer, together with a book and a collection of papers.

January 20th

To Mr Sharpe,
As you may have guessed, you are not dealing with an ordinary theft. The thieves are members of a sinister organization called the Cafelors. This organization has sent the thieves to four foreign cities. In each of the cities they will go to a secret rendezvous where they will hand over one of the Faymus Treasures to their accomplices. I have been able to gather information about the handovers and I have noted everything down on the documents enclosed with this letter.

Yours in haste,

An Informer

P.S. Do not attempt to find out who I am or how I have obtained this information.

THE CITY OF SAN SERIF

MARCATO MANSION

Not in the city of Kastler. Not the handover point for treasure ♡

Z6

ADMIT ONE

Hotel Aurora

not to be confused with the Lady Aurora steamer which is also a handover point

Handover point

Treasure ♡ is to be handed over one month before treasure ◊

The City of Ehrhardt

Handover here two months before handover in Kastler

At a secret meeting on January 1st, the Grand Council of the Cafelors made the following decisions:

1. Ξ and Ω will hand over treasures ♡, ♧, ♤ and ◊ to accomplices at four separate locations, all in different cities. The handovers will take place on the 28th of each month from January to April.

2. Ψ and △ are highly congratulated on their success in tracing the Jesting Figure. They will now join Ξ and Ω on Operation Faymus.

3. ♈ and φ will co-ordinate Operation Dancer. The operation will target the Dancing Figure, which has been out of our hands since the Heliotropic Fiasco 150 years ago.

According to Percival's informer, the thieves have been ordered to go to four foreign cities. At a secret location in each city they will hand over one of the stolen Faymus Treasures to their accomplices. With the help of the parcel's contents, Percival can find out the date and location of the handover for each of the treasures.

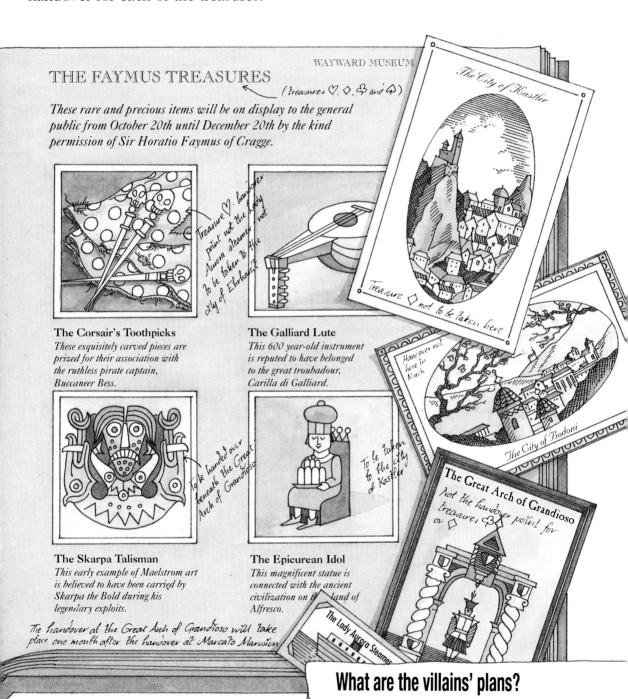

WAYWARD MUSEUM

THE FAYMUS TREASURES

← (treasures ♡, ◊, ♧ and ♤)

These rare and precious items will be on display to the general public from October 20th until December 20th by the kind permission of Sir Horatio Faymus of Cragge.

Treasure ♡ - handover point not the Lady Aurora steamer. To be taken to the city of Ehrharst

The Corsair's Toothpicks
These exquisitely carved pieces are prized for their association with the ruthless pirate captain, Buccaneer Bess.

The Galliard Lute
This 600 year-old instrument is reputed to have belonged to the great troubadour, Carilla di Galliard.

To be handed over beneath the Great Arch of Grandioso

To be taken to the city of Kastler

The Skarpa Talisman
This early example of Maelstrom art is believed to have been carried by Skarpa the Bold during his legendary exploits.

The Epicurean Idol
This magnificent statue is connected with the ancient civilization on the land of Alfresco.

The handover at the Great Arch of Grandioso will take place one month after the handover at Marcato Mansion.

The City of Kastler

Treasure ◊ not to be taken here

Handover not here in March

The City of Bodoni

The Great Arch of Grandioso

Not the handover point for treasures ♧ or ◊

The Lady Aurora Steamer

What are the villains' plans?

A Game of Kaballo

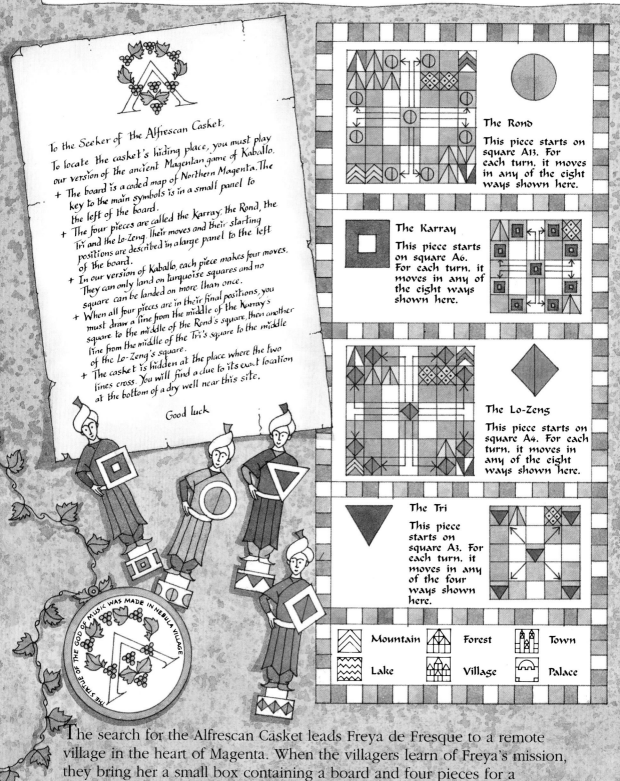

To the Seeker of the Alfrescan Casket,

To locate the casket's hiding place, you must play our version of the ancient Magentan game of Kaballo.

+ The board is a coded map of Northern Magenta. The key to the main symbols is in a small panel to the left of the board.

+ The four pieces are called the Karray, the Rond, the Tri and the Lo-Zeng. Their moves and their starting positions are described in a large panel to the left of the board.

+ In our version of Kaballo, each piece makes four moves. They can only land on turquoise squares and no square can be landed on more than once.

+ When all four pieces are in their final positions, you must draw a line from the middle of the Karray's square to the middle of the Rond's square, then another line from the middle of the Tri's square to the middle of the Lo-Zeng's square.

+ The casket is hidden at the place where the two lines cross. You will find a clue to its exact location at the bottom of a dry well near this site.

Good luck

THE STATUE OF THE GOD OF MUSIC WAS MADE IN NEBULA VILLAGE

The Rond

This piece starts on square A13. For each turn, it moves in any of the eight ways shown here.

The Karray

This piece starts on square A6. For each turn, it moves in any of the eight ways shown here.

The Lo-Zeng

This piece starts on square A4. For each turn, it moves in any of the eight ways shown here.

The Tri

This piece starts on square A3. For each turn, it moves in any of the four ways shown here.

Mountain   Forest   Town

Lake   Village   Palace

The search for the Alfrescan Casket leads Freya de Fresque to a remote village in the heart of Magenta. When the villagers learn of Freya's mission, they bring her a small box containing a board and four pieces for a Magentan game called Kaballo, together with a pendant and a letter.

The letter explains that the brightly patterned board is a disguised map of Northern Magenta. If Freya moves the four Kaballo pieces around the board in a particular way, she will be able to locate the casket's hiding place.

Where is the casket hidden?

The Fort of Skulls

When the Albatross reaches the pirates' island, Peg Traherne swims ashore. As the pirates prepare to set out to sea, Peg hides in a tumbledown shack. Inside she is amazed to discover a collection of papers belonging to Obadiah Walrus. These include two pages from his diary and a plan of the pirates' base, the Fort of Skulls. Peg discovers that Obadiah managed to escape from the pirates, only to be recaptured during a bid to rescue ten fellow prisoners. Using the plan and the information in the diary, Peg can find a safe route to the prisoners' chamber.

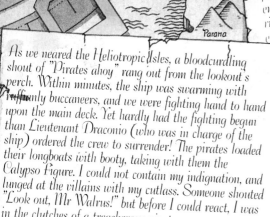

The Statue of the God of Jests was made in Octana village

Persimmon Isle

Saskatoon Isle

Parana

As we neared the *Heliotropic Isles,* a bloodcurdling shout of *"Pirates ahoy"* rang out from the lookout's perch. Within minutes, the ship was swarming with ruffianly buccaneers, and we were fighting hand to hand upon the main deck. Yet hardly had the fighting begun than Lieutenant Draconio (who was in charge of the ship) ordered the crew to surrender! The pirates loaded their longboats with booty, taking with them the *Calypso Figure.* I could not contain my indignation, and lunged at the villains with my cutlass. Someone shouted *"Look out, Mr Walrus!"* but before I could react, I was in the clutches of a treacherous pirate.

The pirates took me to their fortress, but I bribed one of them to help me escape. He gave me a plan of the fort and released me from the *Prisoners' Chamber.*

The next day, however, I was determined to re-enter the fort so that I could release the other wretched captives. I waited until sunset, then slipped inside the fort through an unguarded entrance. I followed the corridor straight in front of me, then darted through the first door on my left whereupon I found myself in the *Torture Chamber.* I crept out through the same door and turned left into the corridor once more. I slipped through the first door on the right, and found myself in the *Gunroom.*

I continued to explore the fort, fearful at every moment lest I should collide with a fierce buccaneer, until I entered the pirates' *Sleeping Quarters.* I crossed

the room then opened a door which took me straight into a larger room which I identified as the *Kitchens.* At that moment I heard the shouts and oaths of approaching pirates, and hastily retreated. I cannot remember my route, but at last I took refuge in a large fireplace in the *Granary.* When I judged it safe to emerge, I returned to the corridor. This time, I turned right, then took the first door on the left, whereupon I entered the *Banqueting Hall.* After that I cannot remember my route, but I know that at some point I passed the *Private Den of Buccaneer Bess,* where all the pirates had assembled and were indulging in devilish merriment; and later I passed by the door of the *Prisoners' Chamber,* a smaller room.

At that moment, I was spotted by a fiery pirate, who came charging toward me, cutlass at the ready. I ran as fast as I could, dodging through the great fortress until I came to the *Private Room of Barebones Jake.* I crossed the room, burst through the door into a corridor, turned left and flung myself through the first door on the right. I was in the *Gunpowder Room,* which I knew concealed the entrance to a secret tunnel. Just as a group of pirates burst into the room, I found the tunnel entrance and made my escape.

Mercifully, in all my wanderings I managed to avoid the devilish booby traps of *Buccaneer Bess.*

All this took place yesterday. Today I shall try my luck once more but this is indeed a perilous mission and I know not if I will succeed.

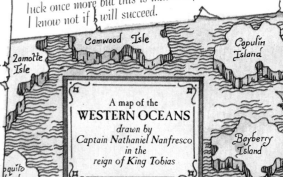

Camwood Isle

Lamotte Isle

Capulín Island

...quito ...land

A map of the
WESTERN OCEANS
drawn by
Captain Nathaniel Nanfresco
in the
reign of King Tobias

Bayberry Island

...Island

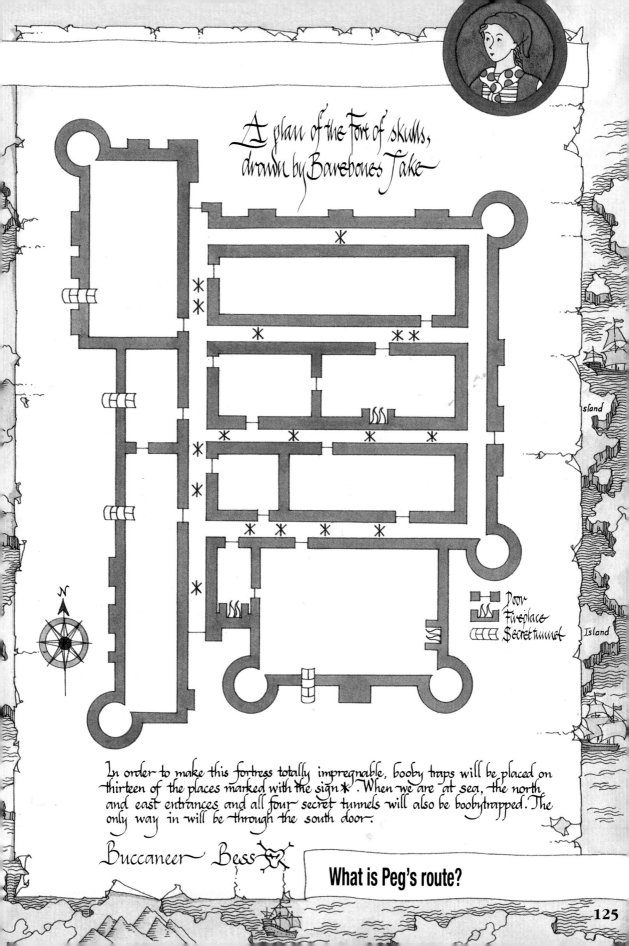

A plan of the Fort of skulls, drawn by Barebones Jake

In order to make this fortress totally impregnable, booby traps will be placed on thirteen of the places marked with the sign ✱. When we are at sea, the north and east entrances and all four secret tunnels will also be boobytrapped. The only way in will be through the south door.

Buccaneer Bess

What is Peg's route?

The Fair of Farrago

According to Aurora the Guardian of Secrets, the statue of the Cantador is hidden in the Amethyst Cave in the land of Magenta. The only person who knows the way to the cave is the Guardian's loyal pageboy, Blondel, who has gone to the Fair of Farrago on Magenta's border. The Guardian explains that Blondel will disguise himself as a different stallholder on each day of the fair.

This tapestry shows the Annual Fair of Farrago.
By the fair's ancient custom, each stall displays a flag and two shields. Each shield is divided into halves.
When the fair first began, each flag had a number and each shield had two numbers, one in each half. The numbers followed a rule. If the two numbers on the right-hand shield were multiplied together and the result was added to the sum of the two numbers on the left-hand shield, the result was the number on the flag.
As time passed, many of these numbers were lost and the number patterns were left incomplete.

Carilla must follow Blondel to the fair and identify each of his disguises. If she can find the pageboy on the last day of the fair, he will lead her to the Cantador's hiding place. This bright tapestry shows the stalls at the Fair of Farrago, together with all the information Carilla needs to reach the end of her quest.

On each of the five days of the fair, Blondel will be disguised as a different stallholder. He has chosen five stalls whose numbers form five sequences. The first sequence links the numbers in the top halves of the stalls' left-hand shields. The second links the numbers in the lower halves of these shields. The third links the numbers in the top halves of the right-hand shields. The fourth links the numbers in the lower halves of these shields. The numbers displayed on the flags of the five stalls form the final sequence. The number displayed on the flag of Blondel's first stall should be 17. The number on one of the shields on the final stall should be 13.

What are Blondel's disguises?

The Final Rendezvous

After recovering three of the stolen Faymus Treasures, Percival Sharpe arrives at the final handover point. Here he finds an envelope from his mysterious informer. Its contents reveal that the location of this handover has been changed in a last minute attempt to throw Percival off the trail.

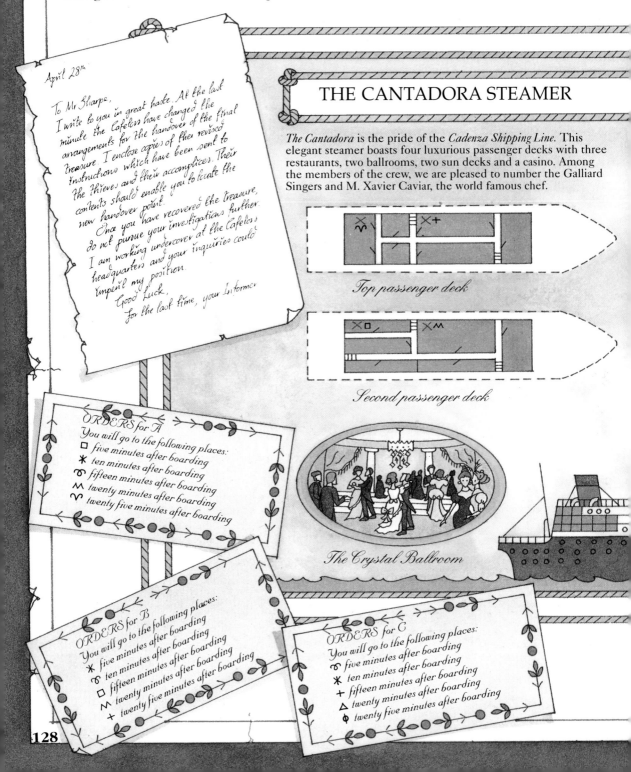

April 28th

To Mr Sharpe,

I write to you in great haste. At the last minute the Cafelars have changed the arrangements for the handover of the final treasure. I enclose copies of their revised instructions which have been sent to the thieves and their accomplices. Their contents should enable you to locate the new handover point.

Once you have recovered the treasure, do not pursue your investigations further. I am working undercover at the Cafelars headquarters and your inquiries could imperil my position.

Good Luck,

For the last time, your Informer

THE CANTADORA STEAMER

The Cantadora is the pride of the Cadenza Shipping Line. This elegant steamer boasts four luxurious passenger decks with three restaurants, two ballrooms, two sun decks and a casino. Among the members of the crew, we are pleased to number the Galliard Singers and M. Xavier Caviar, the world famous chef.

Top passenger deck

Second passenger deck

The Crystal Ballroom

ORDERS for A
You will go to the following places:
□ five minutes after boarding
✳ ten minutes after boarding
ℭ fifteen minutes after boarding
ℳ twenty minutes after boarding
ʒ twenty five minutes after boarding

ORDERS for B
You will go to the following places:
✳ five minutes after boarding
ℭ ten minutes after boarding
□ fifteen minutes after boarding
ℳ twenty minutes after boarding
+ twenty five minutes after boarding

ORDERS for C
You will go to the following places:
ℭ five minutes after boarding
✳ ten minutes after boarding
+ fifteen minutes after boarding
△ twenty minutes after boarding
φ twenty five minutes after boarding

According to the revised arrangements, the thieves will hand over the treasure to their accomplices during one of four meetings aboard the Cantadora steamer at the port of Cadenza. Percival must use information from his informer to discover exactly when and where this meeting will take place.

"Luxury, Serenity, Conviviality"

From the classical restraint of the *Crystal Ballroom* to the exuberant opulence of the *Imperial Restaurant*, every aspect of the Cantadora is finely crafted for the passenger's delight. Those who wish to experience the voyage of a lifetime are requested to write to Captain Draconio, c/o *Cadenza Shipping Line*, Cadenza.

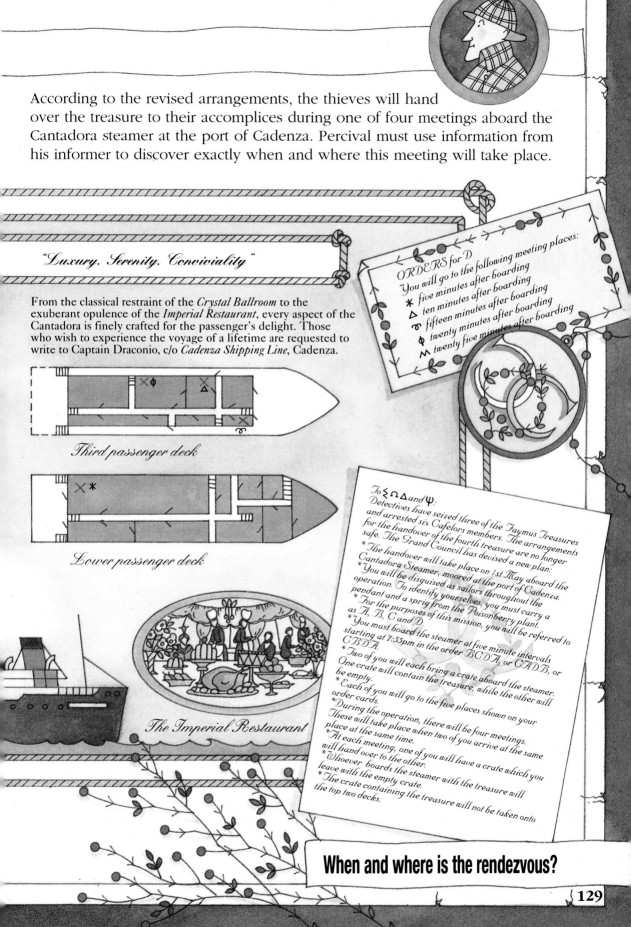

Third passenger deck

Lower passenger deck

The Imperial Restaurant

ORDERS for D
You will go to the following meeting places:
* five minutes after boarding
△ ten minutes after boarding
ℛ fifteen minutes after boarding
φ twenty minutes after boarding
♏ twenty five minutes after boarding

To Σ Ω △ and Ψ.
Detectives have seized three of the Faymus Treasures and arrested six Cafelors members. The arrangements for the handover of the fourth treasure are no longer safe. The Grand Council has devised a new plan:
* The handover will take place on 1st May aboard the Cantadora Steamer, moored at the port of Cadenza.
* You will be disguised as sailors throughout the operation. To identify yourselves, you must carry a pendant and a sprig from the Poisonberry plant.
* For the purposes of this mission, you will be referred to as A, B, C and D.
* You must board the steamer at five minute intervals starting at 7:55pm in the order BCDA, or CADB, or CBDA.
* Two of you will each bring a crate aboard the steamer. One crate will contain the treasure, while the other will be empty.
* Each of you will go to the five places shown on your order cards.
* During the operation, there will be four meetings. These will take place when two of you arrive at the same place at the same time.
* At each meeting, one of you will have a crate which you will hand over to the other.
* Whoever boards the steamer with the treasure will leave with the empty crate.
* The crate containing the treasure will not be taken onto the top two decks.

When and where is the rendezvous?

Treasure Hunt

Secret agent Peg Traherne releases Obadiah Walrus and ten fellow prisoners from the Fort of Skulls. Having found the leader of the Society of Alfresco, her mission is over, but her adventures are not yet at an end. Obadiah explains that he was taking a priceless statue called the Calypso Figure to a secret destination. Now this statue has fallen into the pirates' hands. It must be recovered at all costs and Obadiah needs Peg's help.

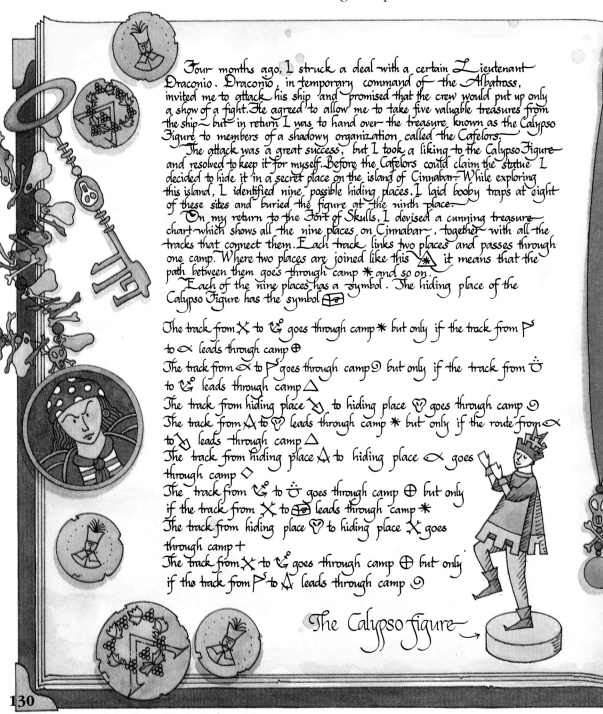

Four months ago, I struck a deal with a certain Lieutenant Draconio. Draconio, in temporary command of the Albatross, invited me to attack his ship and promised that the crew would put up only a show of a fight. He agreed to allow me to take five valuable treasures from the ship — but in return I was to hand over the treasure known as the Calypso Figure to members of a shadowy organization called the Cafelors.

The attack was a great success, but I took a liking to the Calypso Figure and resolved to keep it for myself. Before the Cafelors could claim the statue I decided to hide it in a secret place on the island of Cinnabar. While exploring this island, I identified nine possible hiding places. I laid booby traps at eight of these sites and buried the figure at the ninth place.

On my return to the Fort of Skulls, I devised a cunning treasure chart which shows all the nine places on Cinnabar, together with all the tracks that connect them. Each track links two places and passes through one camp. Where two places are joined like this ⚐ it means that the path between them goes through camp * and so on.

Each of the nine places has a symbol. The hiding place of the Calypso Figure has the symbol 🗋.

The track from X to ꝑ goes through camp * but only if the track from P to ∝ leads through camp ⊕

The track from ∝ to P goes through camp ☉ but only if the track from Ö to ꝑ leads through camp △

The track from hiding place ꝑ to hiding place ♡ goes through camp ☉

The track from A to ♡ leads through camp * but only if the route from ∝ to ꝑ leads through camp △

The track from hiding place A to hiding place ∝ goes through camp ◇

The track from ꝑ to Ö goes through camp ⊕ but only if the track from X to 🗋 leads through camp *

The track from hiding place ♡ to hiding place X goes through camp +

The track from X to ꝑ goes through camp ⊕ but only if the track from P to A leads through camp ☉

The Calypso figure →

While searching the fort, Peg and Obadiah find a secret notebook belonging to the pirate captain. From its contents they learn that the Calypso Figure has been hidden on the island of Cinnabar. The duo must make sense of an ingenious treasure chart to discover which of this island's numerous hiding places conceals the statue. They must search in the right place, or else they will fall foul of the pirates' deadly booby traps.

Where is the Calypso Figure?

The Raider's Fort

The search for the Weather Charm of Wailen Valla leads Skarpa the Bold across the Isle of Doom Laiden to the grim fort of the raider of Maelstrom. On his way, he meets three prisoners who have escaped from the fort. The trio tell Skarpa that the Weather Charm is hidden in a small chest in the raider's treasure chamber. They present him with six clay tablets and a plan of the fort. With the aid of these objects, Skarpa can find a safe route to the treasure chamber, retrieve the stolen charm and return to safety.

PATROL 1

PATROL 2

PATROL 3

PATROL 4

PATROL 5

PATROL 6

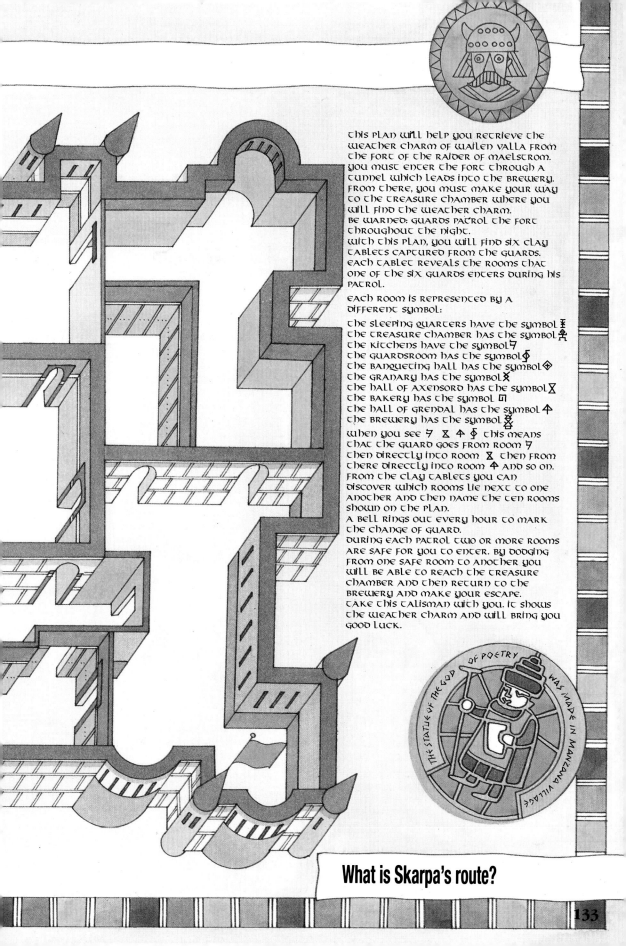

This plan will help you retrieve the weather charm of Wailen Valla from the fort of the raider of Maelstrom. You must enter the fort through a tunnel which leads into the brewery. From there, you must make your way to the treasure chamber where you will find the weather charm.
Be warned: guards patrol the fort throughout the night.
With this plan, you will find six clay tablets captured from the guards. Each tablet reveals the rooms that one of the six guards enters during his patrol.

Each room is represented by a different symbol:

The sleeping quarters have the symbol
The treasure chamber has the symbol
The kitchens have the symbol ⅂
The guardsroom has the symbol ⑂
The banqueting hall has the symbol ◈
The granary has the symbol ⚹
The hall of Axensord has the symbol ⋊
The bakery has the symbol ⒨
The hall of Grendal has the symbol ⯁
The brewery has the symbol ⚡

When you see ⅂ ⚹ ⯁ ⑂ this means that the guard goes from room ⅂ then directly into room ⚹ then from there directly into room ⯁ and so on.
From the clay tablets you can discover which rooms lie next to one another and then name the ten rooms shown on the plan.
A bell rings out every hour to mark the change of guard.
During each patrol two or more rooms are safe for you to enter. By dodging from one safe room to another you will be able to reach the treasure chamber and then return to the brewery and make your escape.
Take this talisman with you. It shows the weather charm and will bring you good luck.

What is Skarpa's route?

The Enigma of the Palace

The trail of the Alfrescan Casket leads Freya de Fresque to a ruined palace high on the plains of Enkantador. On her way she retrieves a small package. This contains a letter and an old painting showing the palace during the reign of King Samerkand. Freya must use the painting to locate the palace's Chamber of Gold and Rubies, for this is where the casket lies hidden.

To the Seeker of the Alfrescan Casket,
The casket is inside the ruined palace on the Plains of Enkantador. It is hidden in a niche above the window of the Chamber of Gold and Rubies. To locate this room, you must use this painting which shows the palace during a visit by the Society of Alfresco eighty years ago.

+ Three of the visitors are on the roof of the palace while in each of the rooms below, one of the other six visitors is shown with a Magentan courtier. Each pair is engaged in a different activity.

+ The names of the visitors are Kappa, Iota, Tau, Gamma, Lambda, Bata, Omega, Zara and Theta.

+ Piece together the information on the right-hand side of the painting to discover which of the rooms is the Chamber of Gold and Rubies.

Good luck, and may the casket restore hope and good fortune to Alfresco.

Dancing

Chess

Feasting

Bathing

Reading

Music

The ruined palace

Neither the Poet, nor the Chief of Ceremonies, nor the Snake Charmer are reading. The Poet is not in the Chamber of the Djinni. Kappa is playing chess. The people in the Peacock Room are either feasting or playing music.
Lambda is not in the same room as the Grand Vizier. Neither the Grand Vizier nor the Snake Charmer are bathing.
Bala is not in the Zebek Room or the Peacock Room. Neither Kappa nor Iota is in the Dragon Room. The Grand Vizier is not in the Zebek Room.
The people in the Zebek Room are not feasting. Gamma is not in the same room as the Chief of Ceremonies.
Iota is not playing music. Lambda is not dancing, bathing, or playing music. Neither the Chief of Ceremonies, nor the Grand Vizier, nor the Snake Charmer are dancing. The Conjuror is not in the Chamber of the Djinni or the Zebek Room. The people in the Dragon Room are not feasting, reading, or playing music.
The Snake Charmer is not in the Chamber of the Five Hundred Candles, the Chamber of the Djinni, or the Peacock Room.

The nine members of the Society of Alfresco were entertained by King Samerkand the Wise. On the fourth day of their visit, the king invited the Alfrescans to his palace on the Plains of Enkantador. This painting shows the king on the palace roof with three of the visitors together with his Chief Falconer and the Court Artist.
Kappa is not in the same room as the Grand Vizier or the Snake Charmer.
The Conjuror is not feasting.
Tau is being entertained by the Acrobat.
Neither the Acrobat nor the Conjurer are in the Dragon Room.
The people in the Chamber of the Djinni are not bathing, playing chess, or feasting.
Lambda is not in the Chamber of Gold and Rubies, nor in the Peacock room. Bala is not in the same room as the Poet or the Chief of Ceremonies.

Which is the Chamber of Gold and Rubies?

135

The Game of Alfresco

The final search for the statues of Alfresco begins when Freya de Fresque retrieves the Alfrescan Casket. The seven ancient statues were stolen by the villainous Cafelors during the Dismal Age of Turmoil and Strife. One of them was later found by Skarpa the Bold and another by Carilla di Galliard, but sadly both were lost again. During the Swashbuckling Age of Buccaneers, the Society of Alfresco was formed to track down the statues and return

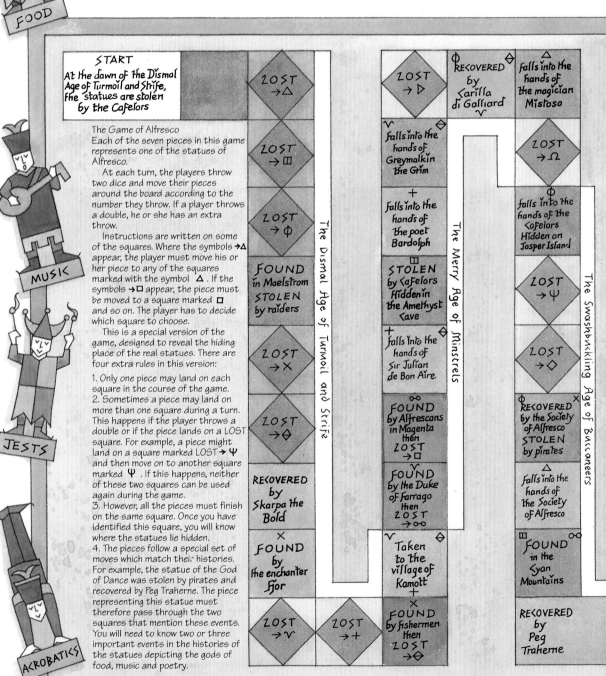

START
At the dawn of the Dismal Age of Turmoil and Strife, the statues are stolen by the Cafelors

The Game of Alfresco
Each of the seven pieces in this game represents one of the statues of Alfresco.

At each turn, the players throw two dice and move their pieces around the board according to the number they throw. If a player throws a double, he or she has an extra throw.

Instructions are written on some of the squares. Where the symbols →△ appear, the player must move his or her piece to any of the squares marked with the symbol △. If the symbols →□ appear, the piece must be moved to a square marked □ and so on. The player has to decide which square to choose.

This is a special version of the game, designed to reveal the hiding place of the real statues. There are four extra rules in this version:

1. Only one piece may land on each square in the course of the game.
2. Sometimes a piece may land on more than one square during a turn. This happens if the player throws a double or if the piece lands on a LOST square. For example, a piece might land on a square marked LOST→ Ψ and then move on to another square marked Ψ. If this happens, neither of these two squares can be used again during the game.
3. However, all the pieces must finish on the same square. Once you have identified this square, you will know where the statues lie hidden.
4. The pieces follow a special set of moves which match their histories. For example, the statue of the God of Dance was stolen by pirates and recovered by Peg Traherne. The piece representing this statue must therefore pass through the two squares that mention these events. You will need to know two or three important events in the histories of the statues depicting the gods of food, music and poetry.

LOST →△

LOST →□

LOST →φ

FOUND in Maelstrom STOLEN by raiders

LOST →✕

LOST →⊕

RECOVERED by Skarpa the Bold

FOUND by the enchanter Fjor

LOST →∨

LOST →+

The Dismal Age of Turmoil and Strife

LOST →▷

falls into the hands of Greymalkin the Grim

✝ falls into the hands of the poet Bardolph

□ STOLEN by Cafelors Hidden in the Amethyst Cave

✝ falls into the hands of Sir Julian de Bon Aire

FOUND by Alfrescans in Magenta then LOST →□

FOUND by the Duke of Farrago then LOST →∞

Taken to the village of Kamott ✝

✕ FOUND by fishermen then LOST →⊕

The Merry Age of Minstrels

φ RECOVERED by Carilla di Galliard ∨

△ falls into the hands of the magician Mistoso

LOST →Ω

φ falls into the hands of the Cafelors Hidden on Jasper Island

LOST →Ψ

LOST →◇

φ RECOVERED by the Society of Alfresco STOLEN by pirates

△ falls into the hands of the Society of Alfresco

□ FOUND in the Cyan Mountains ∞

RECOVERED by Peg Traherne

The Swashbuckling Age of Buccaneers

them to the island. Over the next two centuries its members recovered all seven. However, before the society could return them to the island, the Cafelors blockaded its shores. The statues were hidden by the society and cryptic clues to their location were left inside the Alfrescan Casket. Now the Cafelors have left Alfresco, but no one can make sense of the casket's contents and so find the seven statues.

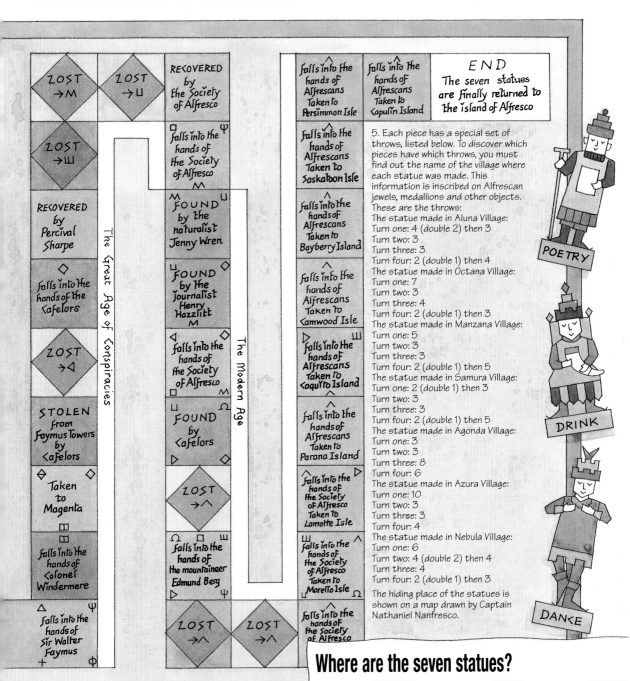

LOST →M

LOST →Ш

LOST →Ш

RECOVERED by the Society of Alfresco

☐ Falls into the hands of the Society of Alfresco Ψ

M FOUND U by the naturalist Jenny Wren

Ш FOUND ◇ by the journalist Henry Hazlitt M

◁ Falls into the hands of the Society of Alfresco ☐ M

Ш FOUND Ω by Cafelors

▷

The Great Age of Conspiracies

RECOVERED by Percival Sharpe

◇ Falls into the hands of the Cafelors

LOST →◁

STOLEN from Faymus Towers by Cafelors

◇ Taken to Magenta ◇

⊞

⊞ Falls into the hands of Colonel Windermere

△ Ψ Falls into the hands of Sir Walter Faymus +   Φ

The Modern Age

LOST →∧

Ω ☐ Ш Falls into the hands of the mountaineer Edmund Berg ▷   Ψ

LOST →∧   LOST →∧

Falls into the hands of Alfrescans Taken to Persimmon Isle

Falls into the hands of Alfrescans Taken to Capulin Island

END The seven statues are finally returned to the island of Alfresco

Falls into the hands of Alfrescans Taken to Saskatoon Isle

Falls into the hands of Alfrescans Taken to Bayberry Island

Falls into the hands of Alfrescans Taken to Camwood Isle

▷ Ш Falls into the hands of Alfrescans Taken to Coquito Island ∧

Falls into the hands of Alfrescans Taken to Parana Island

▷ Falls into the hands of the Society of Alfresco Taken to Lamotte Isle

Ш Falls into the hands of the Society of Alfresco Taken to Morello Isle Ω

∧ Falls into the hands of the Society of Alfresco

5. Each piece has a special set of throws, listed below. To discover which pieces have which throws, you must find out the name of the village where each statue was made. This information is inscribed on Alfrescan jewels, medallions and other objects. These are the throws:
The statue made in Aluna Village:
Turn one: 4 (double 2) then 3
Turn two: 3
Turn three: 3
Turn four: 2 (double 1) then 4
The statue made in Octana Village:
Turn one: 7
Turn two: 3
Turn three: 4
Turn four: 2 (double 1) then 3
The statue made in Manzana Village:
Turn one: 5
Turn two: 3
Turn three: 3
Turn four: 2 (double 1) then 5
The statue made in Samura Village:
Turn one: 2 (double 1) then 3
Turn two: 3
Turn three: 3
Turn four: 2 (double 1) then 5
The statue made in Agonda Village:
Turn one: 3
Turn two: 3
Turn three: 8
Turn four: 6
The statue made in Azura Village:
Turn one: 10
Turn two: 3
Turn three: 3
Turn four: 3
The statue made in Nebula Village:
Turn one: 6
Turn two: 4 (double 2) then 4
Turn three: 4
Turn four: 2 (double 1) then 3
The hiding place of the statues is shown on a map drawn by Captain Nathaniel Nanfresco.

POETRY

DRINK

DANCE

Where are the seven statues?

Clues

Page 100

(1) The easiest way to solve this puzzle is to use a special grid. Here is a simplified version of the puzzle to explain how the grid works. Three characters – Shark, Jonson and Graves – are guarding three entrances of Castle Cloud – the East Tower, the Bell Tower and the North Tower. Each guard is known by a different symbol. One guard is Ψ, another is Ω and the third is Σ.

Shark guards the Bell Tower and is not Ψ. Graves is not Σ. Ψ does not guard the East Tower. Σ does not guard the Bell Tower. Which tower does Jonson guard?

To solve the puzzle, first of all, draw a grid as shown below. Where you know that two things go together, put a tick in the relevant box on the grid. Where you know that two things do not go together, put a cross. With all the information entered, the grid should look like this:

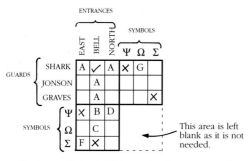

Since Shark guards the Bell Tower, he does not guard the East Tower or the North Tower; and neither Jonson nor Graves guards the Bell Tower, so you can add crosses to the grid in the boxes marked A. You know that Shark guards the Bell Tower and is not Ψ. Therefore the Bell Tower is not guarded by Ψ, so you can put a cross in box B. Since the Bell Tower is not guarded by Σ either, it must be guarded by Ω – put a tick in box C.

Ψ does not guard the Bell Tower and does not guard the East Tower either, so he guards the North Tower – put a tick in box D. In turn, this means that Σ guards the East Tower – put a tick in box F.

The Bell Tower is guarded by Ω and by Shark, so Shark is Ω – put a tick in box G. Can you identify Jonson's symbol? What about Graves's? Your grid should now look like this:

	EAST	BELL	NORTH	Ψ	Ω	Σ
SHARK	✗	✓	✗	✗	✓	✗
JONSON		✗		✗	✗	✓
GRAVES		✗		✓	✗	✗
Ψ	✗	✗	✓			
Ω	✗	✓	✗			
Σ	✓	✗	✗			

Finally, Ψ guards the North Tower and is Graves, so Graves guards the North Tower. Now you should be able to identify Jonson's Tower.

(2) To solve the puzzle on page 100, you will need to draw a larger grid as there are seven guards, seven entrances and seven symbols. Draw the grid and enter all the information. Remember that Hook guards the South

Tower or the Ghost Tower and is either ⋏ or Ɜ or ▽ or Ω. Neither the South Tower nor the Ghost Tower is guarded by Ɜ ▽ or Ω, so Hook is not Ɜ ▽ or Ω. Therefore, by a process of elimination, Hook is ⋏. Now can you identify Clipper's sign? Next identify Jonson's sign, remembering that he guards either the East Tower or the Old Keep.

Page 101

If Skarpa chose the symbol representing the Vale of Tor in the fourth column, this would exclude all three symbols in the second column, so this symbol must be wrong. What would happen if he chose the Fjord of Eirik in the third column? And what about the Lake of Frija in the second column?

Page 102

(1) First translate the symbols on the emblems into numbers, then piece together the five sequences.

(2) Now discover how the shapes move. Look at the first two emblems. The circle goes from top left to bottom right. The square goes from bottom right to top right. Where do the other shapes move to? Does the symbol in the top left section always move to the bottom right section in the following emblem? Does the symbol in the bottom right section always move to the top right section?

Page 103

(1) Identify the mummer who always tells the truth. Could it be the drummer? (Think carefully about his statement, "I always tell a mixtue of truth and lies"). Could it be the piper? If it is neither, could it be the juggler? (Look for contradictions in her statements.) What about the jester?

(2) Now identify the mummer who always lies. Could it be the juggler? If not, when does the juggler tell the truth? Does this help you find the liar?

(3) Next think very carefully about the drummer's first statement. Is it true or false? If it is false, what does he really say when asked how to find the statue? Would this be true or false? Which road should Carilla take?

(4) How many of the jester's statements are correct?

Pages 104-105

(1) Start with the Forest of Tyre. Could it either of the forests in the middle row? (Remember that the Forest of Tyre is over five days' walk from Lapis Lazuli and from one of the three lakes.) Now can you identify Lake Tirin?

(2) Lake Aral must be one of the two remaining lakes. Knowing this, can you rule out one possibility for the Djinni Mountains? Could the Djinni Mountains be in the middle row? Now can you identify Lake Aral?

Pages 106-107

(1) Start by numbering the islands from one to six (it does not matter which island has which number). Then draw a chart like this:

FLAGS:	1	2	3	4	5	6
ISLAND 1	A					
ISLAND 2						
etc						

(2) In each box, write in the four symbols for the relevant village. For instance, in the box marked A, write in the symbols shown for the village on island 1 with flag 1. Now look at the symbols for the villages with flag 4. How many villages have symbol ⌗? If it is only one,

then ⊞ must be the correct symbol for this village. In turn this means that no other village on the same island has symbol ⊞

Pages 108-109

(1) First label the knights (K1, K2, K3 etc) then label the shields (S1, S2 etc) and the horses (H1, H2 etc).
(2) Now draw a grid as explained in the clue for page 100. Down the side, write the names of the ten knights (Gawain, Fernando, etc), then the horses' numbers (H1 to H10), then the knights' numbers (K1 to K10). Across the top, write in the shields' numbers (S1 to S10), then the knights' numbers, then the horses' numbers.
(3) Remember that if, for instance, K2 is holding S5, then you can put a tick in the K2/S5 box.

Pages 110-111

(1) Draw a grid as explained in the clue for page 100. Down the side of the grid, write the names of the five officers, followed by the ship's supplies, and then the decks. Across the top of the grid, write the names of the five treasures, then the decks, then the ship's supplies.
(2) The Casket of Magenta is not on Kraken's deck, and it is on the Gun Deck. Neither Bosun nor Windlass commands the Gun Deck, so the Casket of Magenta is either on Draconio's or Skurvy's deck. Neither Draconio nor Skurvy commands the deck where the spare sails are stored, so the Casket of Magenta is not on the same deck as the spare sails. Could the Casket of Magenta be on the same deck as the firearms? If not, what does this tell you?

Pages 112-113

(1) Use a grid as explained in the clue for page 100. Down the side of the grid, write the names of the members of the Dodo Club, then the dates on which they left Cragge, then the five means of transport. Across the top, write the names of the guests, then the means of transport, then the dates of departure.
(2) Remember that if Charlie Bounder left three days before Priscilla Prince, this means that Bounder did not leave on the 5th or 7th; and that Priscilla Prince did not leave on the 1st or 2nd.
(3) Spratt arrived at Marshby three days after Johnson. We know that Spratt went by train. If Johnson also went by train, he left three days before Spratt. If Johnson went by road, he left four days before Spratt.
(4) Once you have completed the grid, read the end of Percival's diary entry and the first item on the news cutting to identify the thieves.

Page 114

(1) Start by drawing a diagram of the pavilions like this:

RED FLAG

POSITION 1	POSITION 2	POSITION 3
POSITION 4		POSITION 5

YELLOW FLAG

POSITION 6		POSITION 7
POSITION 8	POSITION 9	POSITION 10

(2) In each of the ten positions, write the first letter of the ten musicians' names. If a musician cannot be in a particular position, cross out the relevant letter.
(3) Which positions could Qat and Korabeth occupy? What about Lalik and Izarin – each has only six possible positions.
(4) Three pairs of musicians are next to one another. Two other musicians (Aramis and Faron) are in the same pavilion but not next to one another. With this in mind, can Korabeth be in position 9? Can Qat be in position 9?
(5) If Aramis and Faron were in the pavilion with the yellow flag, either they would occupy positions 8 and 10,

or one would be in the front row and the other in the back row. Remembering that Qat is in the front row of one or other pavilion, and that three pairs of musicians sit next to one another, could Aramis and Faron be in the pavilion with the yellow flag? Next, discover which pavilion Izarin, Lalik, Haliah and Raban occupy.
(6) Which pavilion does Qat occupy? Can you narrow down the possible positions for Sulah and Balbek – remember they are next to one another. What would happen if Aramis or Faron was in position 2? Next, does Lalik have a cloak? What does this tell you about Aramis? Can Korabeth be in positions 6 or 7? If not, does he have a white turban?

Page 115

Draw a grid, as explained in the clue for page 100. Across the top, write the names of the islands, followed by the landmarks (volcano, hermitage etc). Down the side of the grid, write the names of the different Runaatongs, then the landmarks.

Pages 116-117

Use a grid, as explained in the clue for page 100. Down the side of the grid write the names of the places raided by the Whirlwind, then the years, then the warlords. Across the top, write the names of the forts, then the warlords, then the years.

Pages 118-119

(1) The Tower of Four Winds is across the river from the Tower of Torment, but only if the Tower of Four Winds has a pointed doorway. Assume that the Tower of Four Winds does have a pointed doorway. What are the possible positions for the Tower of Torment? What if the Tower of Four Winds does not have a pointed doorway?
(2) The Tower of Belle is across the river from the Tower of Torment – what are its possible positions? Find another clue that will tell you which position is correct. Next, what would happen if the Tower of Rigadoon was on a hilltop? Once you have tried this out, you should have just three possible positions for this tower. Can you reduce the possible positions for the Tower of Rooks to two?

Pages 120-121

(1) Use a grid as explained in the clue for page 100. Down the side, write the names of the treasures, then the four months, then the symbols and then the handover points. Across the top, write the names of the cities, then the handover points, then the symbols, and then the months.
(2) The handover in Ehrhardt is two months before the one in Kastler. Therefore the handover in Ehrhardt is not in March or April, and the one in Kastler is not in January or February. Refer back to this clue (and others like it) as you solve the puzzle.

Pages 122-123

(1) How many possible routes are there for the Tri?
(2) Remembering that only one piece can land on each square in the course of the game, what are the possible routes for the other three pieces? The Rond has two, the Lo-Zeng has four and the Karray has eight.
(3) What would happen if the Karray used square D12? What about E3? Which piece uses square C7?

Pages 124-125

(1) What does Obadiah's diary tell you about the Granary the Kitchens and the Sleeping Quarters? Each has only three possible positions. What are they?
(2) Which rooms on the plan can be the Gunpowder Room? How does Obadiah get to the Torture Chamber?

Using this information, can you find just three possible positions for this room?

(3) Now look at the way the rooms are linked together. For instance, if the Granary was in the southeast corner of the fort, where would the Banqueting Hall be?

(4) Putting everything together, can you find six different ways of labelling the rooms in the fort?

(5) Now read Buccaneer Bess's note on the plan. Remembering that Obadiah avoided the pirates' booby-traps, which of the six combinations is correct?

Pages 126-127

(1) Fill in the gaps on the stalls where only one number is missing. Now draw a chart. At the top, write out the numbers on the flags, from the smallest to the largest. Beneath each flag number, write out the shield numbers (where you know them) for the relevant stall. Now look for possible patterns in the shield numbers. You should find two or three incomplete sequences for each position. Blondel's final stall has the number 13, so one sequence must end with this number. Does this help you identify the correct sequences?

Pages 128-129

(1) Start by drawing a chart, as indicated here:

	Boarding order 1				Boarding order 2				Boarding order 3			
TIME	B	C	D	A	C	A	D	B	C	B	D	A
7:55												
8:00	✳											
8:05	♄											
ETC												

(2) Looking at the cards, you can see that if B was the first to board, he would be at point ✳ at 8:00 (five minutes after boarding), at point ♄ at 8:05 and so on. Add this information to the chart (it has been started for you), then do the same for the other Cafelors members. Next do the same for the other boarding orders.

(3) A meeting takes place when two Cafelors are in the same place at the same time. Where would the meetings be if the villains boarded in order 1? Who would be involved? What about orders 2 and 3? (Two meetings can take place at the same time.)

(4) There are two crates, and one crate is to be handed over at each meeting. At the first meeting, there are four possible scenarios. If the meeting is between A and D, then either A hands the crate with the treasure to D; or D hands this crate to A; or A hands the empty crate to D; or D hands the empty crate to A.

Assume that D hands the empty crate to A at the first meeting, and that the second meeting is between C and D. At this meeting, C must hand the crate with the treasure to D. If the meeting was between C and A, A would hand the empty crate to C. Using similar reasoning, figure out all the scenarios for the different boarding orders.

(5) Remember that the person who boards with the treasure will leave with the empty crate.

(6) Finally, figure out which decks the genuine crate would be taken to in each possibility. Remember to include the places the crate is taken to between meetings.

Pages 130-131

(1) Draw a chart to show the routes between the different hiding places as indicated here.

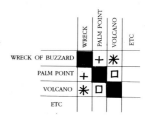

	WRECK	PALM POINT	VOLCANO	ETC
WRECK OF BUZZARD		+	✳	
PALM POINT	+		□	
VOLCANO	✳	□		
ETC				

(2) Draw a grid with the names of the hiding places down the side, and their symbols along the top. If you discover, for instance, that ☝ is not the Devil's Cave, put a cross in the relevant box. If you discover that ☝ is the Devil's Cave, put a tick in that box.

(3) The track from ⑦ to ✗ goes through +. Look at the chart. How many hiding places are joined by a track going through + ? The track from ♄ to ⑦ goes through ◔. You should have only two possibilities for ⑦. What are the possibilities for ♄?

(4) The track from ⋏ to ⑦ goes through ✳ but only if the track from ∝ to ♄ goes through △ . ♄ has two possibilities; ∝ has seven. With these possibilities in mind, can the track from ♄ to ∝ go through ✳?

Pages 132-133

(1) From the clay tablets, you know that, for instance, a door leads from ⊠ into ◈ ⫟ ⅂ and ⅄ . ⊠ must therefore have at least four doors. Draw a chart showing each room, its minimum number of doors and which rooms it is next to.

(2) There is one room in the fort with only one door. This has to be either ⅄ or ⅂. What would happen if it was ⅂ ?

(3) Once you have identified the room with one door, you can easily identify the room next to it. Now what do you know about the positions of ⫟ ⅄⫟ and ◈? And what about ⊠ ◻ ⅂ and ⅄ ? Next identify the room with two doors. There are now only two possibilities. Which is correct? Having identified all ten rooms, look at the clay tablets again. Which rooms are safe during each patrol?

Pages 134-135

(1) Draw a grid as described in the clue for page 100. Down the side write the names of the guests, then the names of the courtiers, then the rooms. Across the top, write the activities, then the rooms, then the courtiers.

(2) Lambda is either reading or feasting. Assume that he is feasting. Is this possible? Once you know, find out which courtier is reading, then which activity is taking place in the Chamber of the Five Hundred Candles. You should now know that either the poet or the acrobat is dancing. Assume that it is the poet. Is this possible?

Pages 136-137

To find out which set of throws belongs to each piece, look back through the book to discover where each statue was made. Each piece follows a set of moves that matches its history. Which two squares must the god of poetry use? (The statue may have more than one name – look at page 133.) Which two squares must the god of dance use? (Again, the statue has more than one name – look at pages 115 and 130.) Can you find three squares for the god of food? (For its other name, look at page 121.) Now you are ready to start playing the game. Start by numbering the squares from 1 to 60. Then write out all the possible routes for each piece, remembering that if, for instance, square 21 is used by the piece representing the god of music, it cannot be used by any other piece. Some pieces have more than fifteen routes! Next, decide which piece uses square 33. Then look at 13, 19, 18, 14, 48, 32 and 15 in turn. Now what are the possible end squares? (There should be three.) Try each in turn - which is correct?

Answers

Page 100

From the letter, Peg knows that the safe entrance is the one guarded by Morgrim.
Piecing together the information supplied by the Society of Alfresco, she makes the following discoveries:

Shark is ∅ and guards the South Tower
Smythe is ⋝ and guards the Old Keep
Hook is ⋏ and guards the Ghost Tower

Graves is ∇ and guards the North Tower
Clipper is ∋ and guards the Bell Tower
Jonson is Ω and guards the East Tower
Morgrim is Ψ and guards the Great Hall

Peg should therefore use the entrance to the Great Hall.

Page 101

Skarpa should choose the symbols ringed here:

The five perilous places he will encounter on the way to the Hall of Fire and Ice are therefore the Castle of Knutt, the Castle of Giants, the Cave of Kromm, the Valley of Eadric and the Grove of Grendel.

Page 102

From the villains' letter, Percival knows that he must find five hidden number sequences. These are:

Circle: 1 (✚) 2 (Ψ) 4 (δ) 8 (U) 16 (✕)

Triangle: 10 (M) 8 (U) 6 (θ) 4 (δ) 2 (Ψ)

Pentagon: 15 (M) 12 (Λ) 9 (?) 6 (θ) 3 (V)

Square: 1 (✚) 3 (V) 5 (Q) 7 (K) 9 (?)

Diamond: 2 (Ψ) 3 (V) 5 (Q) 8 (U) 12 (Λ)

The shapes move around the emblems following the arrows on this diagram:

Putting all this together, Percival discovers that the sequence is:

Percival knows that the thieves were staying at the house with the fourth emblem. This is shown here.

Page 103

Carilla deduces that the bear always tells the truth, the drummer always lies and the other mummers tell a mixture of truth and lies. To discover which road to take, Carilla has to think very carefully about the drummer's first statement. The drummer always lies, so the statement is false. This means that if Carilla asked him directly which road she should take to find the statue, he would NOT reply, "You must take the road to the town of Tabor". He would actually reply, "You must take the road to Mandolin". This would itself be a lie, so Carilla must head for Tabor. Carilla must therefore head for Tabor; at the crossroads she should go to the Castle of Arc, where she should find the cook.

Pages 104-105

The names of the forests, lakes and mountains are shown here. Freya's route is marked in black.

Mountains of Nadir — Lake Aral — Forest of Okra — Zephyr Mountains — Forest of Tyre
Djinni Mountains
Cyan Mountains
Lapis Lazuli
Lake Tirin
Forest of Jakal
Forest of Sesame — Lake Laq

Pages 106-107

This is the village of Kamott

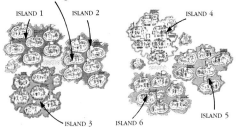

The following chart shows the secret signs of all the villages in the Runik Isles:

FLAGS:	1	2	3	4	5	6
ISLAND 1						
ISLAND 2						
ISLAND 3						
ISLAND 4						
ISLAND 5						
ISLAND 6						

Pages 108-109

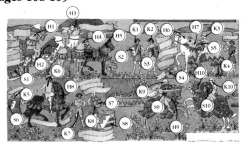

Piecing all the information together, Carilla can name all ten knights and identify their horses and shields:
Sir Gerard is K2. His horse is H4 and his shield is S3
Sir Fernando is K3. His horse is H7 and his shield is S5
Sir Caspar is K8. His horse is H1 and his shield is S7
Sir Almeric is K6. His horse is H8 and his shield is S1
Sir Emilio is K5. His horse is H6 and his shield is S6
Sir Harold is K4. His horse is H2 and his shield is S8
Sir Gawain is K7. His horse is H3 and his shield is S4
Sir Balthus is K10. His horse is H10 and his shield is S10
Sir Sigismund is K1. His horse is H5 and his shield is S2
Sir Jules is K9. His horse is H9 and his shield is S9

Pages 110-111

To identify Draconio's deck, Peg pieces together all the information on the plan of the ship. This is what she discovers:
Kraken commands the Lower Deck, where the Goldenhall Talisman and the spare sails are stored.
Skurvy commands the Gun Deck, where the Casket of Magenta and the ropes are stored.
Bosun commands the Quarterdeck, where the Tamarind Jewels and the ship's biscuits are stored.
Windlass commands the Poop Deck, where the Galliard Lute and the rum are stored.
Draconio commands the Main Deck, where the Calypso Figure and the firearms are stored.
Therefore the missing logbook is hidden on the Main Deck.

Pages 112-113

From the scattered pieces of information, Percival comes to the following conclusions:
Robert Johnson left Cragge with Jonathon Sutch by stagecoach on the 1st, arriving in Marshby on the 3rd.
Charlie Bounder left Cragge with Maria Jones on the Piston Express on the 2nd, arriving in Marshby on the 3rd.
The Marchioness of Rotunda left Cragge with Denholm Hazzlitt by carriage on the 4th, arriving in Marshby on the 6th.
Jacob Spratt left Cragge with Priscilla Prince on the Gantry Express on the 5th, arriving in Marshby on the 6th.
Lucinda Eliot left Cragge with Fanny Wren by hansom on the 7th, arriving in Marshby on the 9th.
Percival knows that the thieves, a man and a woman, stayed at the Swan Inn in Marshby. According to the newscutting, the inn was closed from January 6th to January 8th. The only man and woman to arrive in Marshby together when the inn was open are Charlie Bounder and Maria Jones. They must therefore be the thieves.

Page 114

Freya knows that she must go to the village of the musician, Aramis. Piecing together the information at the top of the painting, she is able to name all the musicians:

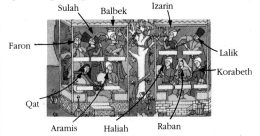

Sulah, Balbek, Izarin, Faron, Lalik, Korabeth, Qat, Aramis, Haliah, Raban

The names of the musicians' villages are written on their music stands. Aramis's village is Turmeric. This is where Freya should go next.

Page 115

From the "Wanted" poster, Peg knows that the pirates live in a fort built on the ruins of an ancient palace. To locate this palace, she has to piece together all the information in the documents. This is what she discovers: the Rufus Runaatong and the mango groves are on Jaspar Island; the Long-Tailed Runaatong and the swamps are on Eastern Island; the Klamorus Runaatong and the standing stones are on Corallina Island; the Short-Haired Runaatong and the hermitage are on Salamander Isle; the Howling Runaatong and the tower are on the Isle of Parakeets; the Silver-Haired Runaatong and the volcano are on Solferino Island; the Bouncing Runaatong and the ancient palace are on Cinnabar Island.

Therefore the pirates are based on Cinnabar Island.

Pages 116-117

To discover which fort he should search, Skarpa must first name the warlord who raided Maelstrom. From the information on the stone, Skarpa makes the following discoveries:

Erik the Mighty raided Vidar in the Year of the Storms. He lives in the Fort of High Towers.

Harold the Hardy raided Alfresco in the Year of the Mighty Seamonster. He lives in the North Fort.

Gunhilde the Ruthless raided Lilla Vaga in the Year of the Great Curse. She lives in the South Fort.

Sombrik the Proud raided Loki in the Year of the Midnight Sun. He lives in the Fort of Blackstone.

Knutt the Fearsome raided Maelstrom in the Year of the Heroic Sea Voyage. He lives in the Fort of the Dragonstone.

Skarpa should therefore search the Fort of the Dragonstone.

Pages 118-119

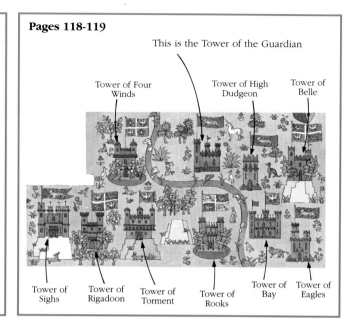

This is the Tower of the Guardian

Tower of Four Winds

Tower of High Dudgeon

Tower of Belle

Tower of Sighs

Tower of Rigadoon

Tower of Torment

Tower of Rooks

Tower of Bay

Tower of Eagles

Pages 120-121

From the informer's notes, Percival can deduce exactly what the villains are planning to do:

In January, the Corsair's Toothpicks (♡) will be taken to Hotel Aurora in Bodoni

In February, the Galliard Lute (◊) will be taken to Marcato Mansion in Ehrhardt

In March, the Skarpa Talisman ♠) will be taken to the Great Arch of Grandioso in San Serif

In April, the Epicurean Idol (♣) will be taken to the Lady Aurora Steamer in Kastler

Pages 122-123

To locate the hiding place of the Alfrescan Casket, Freya must figure out the moves of the four pieces in the special version of Kaballo. The moves are as follows:

Tri:	A3	C5	E7	C9	E11
Rond:	A13	D12	G11	H8	I5
Lo-Zeng:	A4	D2	B5	E3	B1
Karray:	A6	B4	D5	C7	B9

Following the instructions in the letter, Freya therefore draws one line from B9 to I5 and another from B1 to E11. The lines cross in square D8, which shows a palace. This is where the Alfrescan Casket is hidden.

Pages 124-125

Peg's route to the Prisoners' Chamber is shown in black.

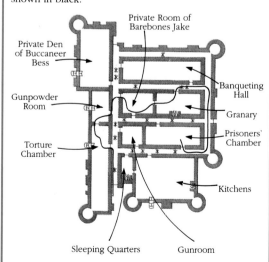

Private Room of Barebones Jake

Private Den of Buccaneer Bess

Gunpowder Room

Banqueting Hall

Granary

Prisoners' Chamber

Torture Chamber

Kitchens

Sleeping Quarters

Gunroom

Pages 126-127

Carilla knows that she must find five hidden number sequences to identify the stalls where Blondel will appear during the fair. First, she fills in the blanks on stalls where only one number is missing. Then, piecing this information together, she identifies two or three possible number sequnces for each of the four positions on the shields. Fitting these together, she arrives at the correct sequences. These are:

Left-hand shield, top: 1 4 7 10 13
Left-hand shield, bottom: 3 5 7 9 11
Right-hand shield, top: 10 12 14 16 18
Right-hand shield, bottom: 4 6 8 10 12
Flags: 17 38 71 116 173 (the difference between these numbers increases by 12 each time)

Blondel will therefore appear disguised as the following stallholders:
Day 1: Juggler
Day 2: The owner of the Dragon of Drumm
Day 3. The magician Mistoso
Day 4: The owner of Frommerty's Hearty Victuals
Day 5: Doctor Quack

Pages 128-129

From the information provided by the informer, Percival is able to deduce exactly what the villains are planning to do. They will board the steamer in the order CBDA. At the first meeting (8:05), C will hand the empty crate to B at place ✳. At the second meeting (8:15) D will hand the crate with the treasure to C at place △ At the third meeting (also 8:15), B will hand the empty crate to A at place □ At the fourth meeting (8:30) A will hand the empty crate to D at place M Percival should therefore intercept the meeting at place △ at 8:15.

Pages 130-131

From the secret notebook, Peg and Obadiah know that each of the nine hiding places on Cinnabar Island has been given a secret symbol and that the statue is hidden at place 🗝. Piecing together the information in the notebook, they match each hiding place to its symbol:

Palm Point is ⚔

The Wreck of the Buzzard is ♙

The Jaggid Rocks are ◁

The Dolmen Stone is ⚓

The Watchtower is ☋

The Great Falls are ⚑

The Volcano is 🜍

The Devil's Cave is ◈

The Blue Mountain is 🗝

The Calypso Figure is therefore hidden on the Blue Mountain.

Pages 132-133

First of all Skarpa names all the rooms in the fort:

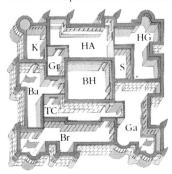

S = Sleeping Quarters
TC = Treasure Chamber
K = Kitchens
Ga = Guardsroom
BH = Banqueting Hall
Gr = Granary
HA = Hall of Axensord
Ba = Bakery
HG = Hall of Grendal
Br = Brewery

This is his route:
Br-Ba-K (during patrol 1); K-Gr (during patrol 2); Gr-BH (during patrol 3); BH-TC-Ba-K (during patrol 4); K-Gr (during patrol 5); Gr-Ba-Br (during patrol 6)

Pages 134-135

Freya knows that the casket is hidden in the Chamber of Gold and Rubies. To locate this room, she pieces together all the information on the right-hand side of the painting. This is what she discovers:

Kappa and the Chief of Ceremonies are playing chess in the Zebek Room
Gamma and the Poet are bathing in the Dragon Room
Tau and the Acrobat are dancing in the Djinni Room
Lambda and the Conjurer are reading in the Chamber of the Five Hundred Candles
Iota and the Grand Vizier are feasting in the Peacock Room
Bala and the Snake Charmer are playing music in the Chamber of Gold and Rubies

The Chamber of Gold and Rubies is therefore the room marked "Music" in the painting.

Pages 136-137

To find the statues, you must discover the moves that each of the seven pieces makes in the Games of Alfresco. To do this you need the following information: the statue of the god of poetry (also known as the Weather Charm of Wailen Valla) was stolen from Maelstrom, then later recovered by Skarpa the Bold; the statue of the god of dance (also known as the Calypso Figure) was stolen by pirates and recovered by Peg Traherne; the statue of the god of food (also known as the Epicurean Idol) fell into the hands of Horatio Faymus, then was stolen from Faymus Towers, later to be recovered by Percival Sharpe. From page 40, you also know the statue of the god of music was hidden in the Amethyst Cave, then retrieved by Carilla di Galliard.

Remembering that only one piece may land on each square in the course of the game, and that all seven pieces finish on the same square, you can now deduce the moves for each piece:

Dance (made in Aluna Village): 4 24 27 30 33 35 43 47 58
Jests (made in Octana Village): 7 19 22 26 36 38 55 58
Poetry (made in Manzana Village): 5 8 11 18 20 53 58
Food (made in Samura Village): 2 28 31 34 37 39 45 50 58
Acrobatics (made in Agonda Village): 3 29 32 40 52 58
Drink (made in Azura Village): 10 14 15 48 51 54 58
Music (made in Nebula Village): 6 9 13 17 21 23 46 49 58
The statues are therefore hidden on Saskatoon Isle, which is shown on the map of Nathaniel Nanfresco on page 28.

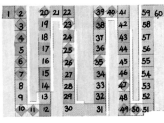

First published in 1994 by Usborne Publishing Ltd, Usborne House, 83-85 Saffron Hill, London EC1N 8RT, England.
Copyright © 1994 Usborne Publishing Ltd.

The name Usborne and the device 🎈 are Trade Marks of Usborne Publishing Ltd.

Printed in Spain   U.E.
First published in America August 1994